## *TWO ROUGH HANDS ROLLED ME OVER AND PRESSED MY FACE INTO THE PILLOW.*

As soon as I was fully awake, I began to struggle. Trussed and gagged, I could scarcely breathe, and any attempt to scream brought on a smothering sensation.... Lonnie lifted me up and threw me over his shoulder. The French doors were open, and by the faint light that came through them I saw Lonnie's nervous friend, Paco, standing at the foot of the bed.

"Check the balcony," Lonnie ordered, and Paco moved to the open doors.

"It's clear," he said, "and there's nobody below."

So that's what they planned! I was to be thrown from my third-floor room to smash like a melon against the stone bridge!

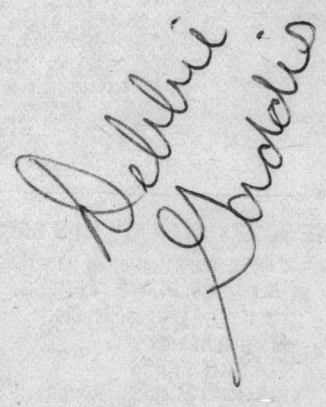

**WE HOPE YOU ENJOY THIS BOOK**
If you'd like a free list of other paperbacks
available from PLAYBOY PRESS,
just send your request to:
**Marilyn Adams
PLAYBOY PRESS
919 North Michigan Avenue
Chicago, Illinois 60611**

(Please enclose 25¢ to help pay for postage and handling.)

# SARA NORTH
# JASMINE FOR MY GRAVE

PLAYBOY PRESS
PAPERBACKS

JASMINE FOR MY GRAVE

*Cover illustration by Sam Thiewes.*

Copyright © 1978 by Playboy. All rights reserved. No part of this book may be reproduced, stored in a retrieval system or transmitted in any form by an electronic, mechanical, photocopying, recording means or otherwise without prior written permission of the author.

Published simultaneously in the United States and Canada by Playboy Press, Chicago, Illinois. Printed in the United States of America. Library of Congress Catalog Card Number: 78-60270. First edition.

Books are available at quantity discounts for promotional and industrial use. For further information, write our sales-promotion agency: Ventura Associates, 40 East 49th Street, New York, New York 10017.

ISBN: 0-872-16494-2

# CHAPTER ONE

One moment the world glittered as if it were wrapped in gold leaf, the next it went black. The nose of my lemon-colored sports car was pushing its way through the sunny, subtropical countryside of San Antonio, past jasmine bushes in full flower, the small yellow blossoms spilling down the drooping branches like a cascade of golden stars, past trees whose leaves appeared gilt-edged in the late afternoon sunlight.

Upon leaving Mission Espada, I had planned to make a leisurely drive past a succession of old Spanish missions before returning to my hotel in the heart of the city, but I had taken the wrong road. I'd had little experience at finding my way around cities, and though I had a map, it was of little use: map reading requires experience, too. I had passed a sign marking the city limits, so at least I was headed in the right direction. And if I became really lost, I could always stop and ask someone the way. Besides, I was enjoying myself. Back home in Nebraska, the February landscape was an unrelieved gray. The lush green and gold San Antonio countryside was balm to my eyes, weary of that colorless world locked in cold.

The road that I followed was a narrow one, winding its way through the trees and shrubs that crowded the roadside. I hadn't seen a house for several miles, when suddenly one rose up before me. Only portions of it were visible behind the thick bamboo hedge and the large trees that stood upon its broad lawn—white stucco walls, tall white chimneys, each one capped with red tile. Intrigued by its size and grandiose Spanish style, I slowed down the car. An asphalt driveway, beyond a gate flanked by two brick pillars, wound up a slight rise to the house. I peered up the drive as I crept past and caught a glimpse of arched windows and doors, trimmed shrubbery against white walls, and red-tiled roofs. The drive, which curved in front of the house, swept down to another gate, a twin to the one I'd just passed. I kept the car at slow speed, hoping to get one more look. This probably saved my life. A car shot out of the second gate as I passed it. My foot flew to the brake. I had a moment's glimpse of a girl's face, white with terror, before our cars met. I felt a jolting impact; then the lovely sun-drenched world went black.

"Are you all right, child? Yes, that's right, open your eyes. Thank God, you're alive!"

I was slumped forward, my head resting on the steering wheel. I sat up slowly and tried to focus my eyes on the stricken face of a gray-haired man.

He had opened the door of my car and was gripping my left arm.

"I—I think I'm all right," I said, shifting my body cautiously. My coordination seemed normal, but my neck was sore, and I discovered a small bump above my right eye where my head had struck the steering wheel.

"Can you walk?"

"I'm not sure," I said groggily and examined the mass of crushed metal and shattered glass that had been the passenger side of my car. The dark sedan stood just beyond the twisted metal. The two cars, thrown about by the impact of the collision, were welded side by side, the crushed side of my car against the driver's side of the other.

"Is the other girl all right?"

"What girl?"

"The one who was driving the other car."

"I was driving the other car, and outside of a few bruises I'm fine. I'm terribly sorry about this. I was in a hurry, you see, and———"

I stared at him as I struggled to remember those last few seconds before the crash. "There was a girl driving that car," I insisted. "I saw her clearly before we collided. She looked scared to death."

The man shook his head. "No, it was I who came shooting down the drive and smashed into your car." A shadow of anxiety settled on his face. "I'm afraid the bump on your head might be more serious than it looks. If you can walk, I'll take you up to the house and call a doctor."

I brushed my hand across my eyes. I was certain a girl had been driving that car. If the blow to my head had so scrambled my brain that I could mistake

him for a girl, then I certainly needed a doctor.
Shaken and frightened, I let the man help me out of
the car. As we walked slowly up the curving drive,
he kept his hand firmly on my elbow. In the center
of the semicircle of lawn bordered by the drive stood
an ancient live oak. Some of its limbs were so long
they had had to be wired and braced to keep them
from breaking under their own weight. Among the
other trees that shaded the carefully tended lawn
on either side of the drive I caught sight of the yellow
fuzz and the sweet fragrance of a huisache tree.
My acquaintance with both trees was very new.
Having arrived in San Antonio the previous afternoon
still early enough to do some sight-seeing, I
left my hotel on the Paseo del Rio and walked to
the Alamo. Its garden held dozens of trees, all conveniently
labeled. Tree lover that I am, I had spent
a delightful hour walking about and studying trees
that were completely unknown to me. I had been
especially captivated by the tiny, perfectly round
fuzzy blossoms of the huisache and by their enchanting
perfume.

The house itself was so unlike the bungalows and
ranch-style houses back home. Its facade looked
aloof, secretive. Only two windows on the second
story broke the blank stretch of white stucco above
the arched windows on the ground floor. The entrance,
set back under an arched portico, was in
shadow. Blinking in the glare of the white walls, I
regarded the closed, unfriendly face of the house
with the uneasy feeling that the doors would have
remained closed to me had it not been for the kindly
man at my side. We entered a wide foyer with glass

doors opposite the entrance. Through these doors I could see a large courtyard. To my right an open stairway curved toward the second floor.

"Come this way, child."

I was shown into a long room to the left of the foyer. The ceiling was so heavily beamed, the furniture so dark and massive, that I entered the room reluctantly. I felt smothered by its weight and silent power. The man helped me to a sofa, which proved surprisingly soft, and I lay down gratefully as he placed a pillow beneath my head.

He went swiftly to the wall beside the fireplace and pressed a button set in a wooden panel. Almost immediately a small, pretty Mexican woman wearing a maid's uniform appeared through one of the two doors at the far end of the living room. "Raphaela, see that this young lady has everything she needs while I call the doctor."

The woman, only a few years older than I, came forward slowly. Her black eyes were wary, her expression anxious, even fearful, it seemed to me. But this wasn't the girl I had seen behind the wheel of the sedan. "Yes, *señorita*," she said with a heavy Spanish accent. "You would like some brandy, or maybe sherry?"

"No, thank you." I didn't want my brain fogged any more than it appeared to be. I went over those few moments before the crash, trying desperately to recall every detail. The picture was absolutely clear in my mind. The girl was young, in her teens, with long blond hair and dark eyes in a pale, frightened face. "The girl who ran into my car," I said, testing, "how is she?"

"I—I do not understand. My English is not so good. If you will not have brandy, perhaps you would like a soft drink or some iced tea?"

"Iced tea sounds wonderful. I was asking about the girl who crashed into my car. She must have been hurt, too."

The maid stared at me with obvious hostility. "There was no girl. *Señor* Stansbury was driving his car. You'll be all right if I leave you to get the iced tea?"

I nodded, relieved to be left alone. When she was gone, I moved my head restlessly on the pillow. Why were they lying to me? Everything was so strange. Even the fireplace was like no other I'd ever seen. The opening was very high and shallow. I could see the remains of last night's fire. The charred logs were not arranged horizontally but stood upright, braced against the rear wall of the firebox.

To the left of the fireplace was a painting, a long canvas in a narrow black wood frame. It was a picture of the Sahara. A camel and a dismounted rider, dwarfed by an infinity of lifeless sand, were the only living things in the picture. The Arab was kneeling, touching his forehead to the sand. There were only two bits of color—the red sandals that the Arab had removed and placed beside him and the narrow ribbon of the same color that appeared along the eastern horizon. There was a presence in the picture, unseen but felt, menacing and cruel in its indifference to the fragment of life kneeling in the sand. I shivered and looked away. At that moment I'd have given anything to be back home, the world around me comfortingly familiar and safe, with my mother fussing over me because I'd been hurt.

"Where is Raphaela," Mr. Stansbury asked when he returned. "I meant for her to stay with you."

"She's getting some iced tea for me." I studied him critically. He was a short, slightly built man with wavy silver hair and a neat mustache. The soft, pink face was definitely not young and just as definitely not feminine. It was impossible that I could have mistaken his face for that of a young girl.

"How are you feeling?" His concern was so genuine, his grandfatherly appearance so reassuring, that my uneasiness began to fade.

"I still feel a bit shaken up, and I have a slight headache. Other than that I seem to be OK."

"I called my doctor. He's not in his office, but his nurse is trying to reach him. He'll be here shortly, I hope. I've also reported the accident to the police and called for a tow truck. I accept full liability. My insurance will take care of everything. You're not to worry about a thing. I'll arrange to have your car repaired or replaced if that should prove necessary."

"That's very generous of you, Mr. Stansbury."

He started. "You know who I am?"

"Raphaela mentioned your name. I'm Libby Kincaid."

"And you are not from Texas," he said, smiling. "Your accent tells me that." He sat down in the chair beside the sofa, legs crossed gracefully, a thin, silken-clad ankle showing above a well-polished shoe.

"I live in Nebraska, in a very small town, population one thousand, surrounded by miles and miles of cornfields and rolling pastures."

"And what has brought you to Texas?"

"A travelogue about San Antonio that was shown

on TV. My girlfriend and I saw it and decided that when we finished business school, we would come here to look for jobs. But then she met a boy she liked too much to leave. So I came alone."

My parents had objected fiercely: "You don't know anything about cities." "You're far too trusting of people." "You've never really been away from home, and now to go so far!"

"I've been away to college," I reminded them.

"Only fifty miles from here, and home every weekend. I don't call that being away."

"Well, it was you who insisted I go to that college. I wanted to go to the University of Colorado."

"You're young for your years. That's partly our fault. We may have been too protective."

My brother, Jack, my elder by eight years and a doctor in a neighboring town, repeated that theme. "Look, Scrub, don't expect to find the world as nice a place as Bedford. Practically everyone here has known you since you were born, and because of your miniaturization they've tended to treat you with the same tolerant amusement they'd show a puppy."

"Thanks a lot, big brother."

"My pleasure. Once you leave here, you're going to be just another human being competing for money, space, and the necessities of life. You're not going to be that 'cute Kincaid kid' out there. They couldn't care less who you are. They'll use you, abuse you, hurt you—if you let them. You can't expect anyone to look out for you except yourself."

"Who'd have thought all these years that under that wholesome all-American-boy exterior was a cynic screaming to get out," I observed dryly.

"I'm not saying you should suspect and distrust everyone you meet, but please regard them with a little suspicion until you find out they can be trusted. Don't make the mistake of believing everyone in the world is your friend just because everyone here in Bedford is. You'll find a lot of people will regard you as an enemy simply because they want the same seat on the bus."

"For Pete's sake, Jack, I know that!"

"OK, so you know a few things. But you've been raised in a pretty controlled environment. There are germs out in the real world, Scrub, and you're sure to come in contact with some of them."

Now Mr. Stansbury echoed the same refrain. "Aren't you awfully young to be on your own?"

"I'm twenty-one," I declared and braced myself for what I knew was coming.

"You look scarcely sixteen!"

"Believe me, it's a darn nuisance. I can't order a drink without being asked to produce identification. If only I could have grown a few more inches!" It was an old lament, one I'd made countless times. My meager height of five feet and my small bones threatened to keep me a juvenile forever in the eyes of other people. "People take one look at me and treat me like a child. It's tiresome."

"Surely it has its advantages," Mr. Stansbury suggested.

At the moment I was inclined to agree. It was a relief to know that he was taking care of all the problems involved in the accident. "Perhaps," I replied as Raphaela arrived with a glass of tea on a tray. I thanked her, and she withdrew without a glance at her employer.

As I took a sip of the tea, which was ice-cold and tasted faintly of mint, I heard voices in the foyer and heels clicking across the polished tile floor. A couple in their thirties entered the room. The woman was striking-looking despite her rather plain face. Her auburn hair was wound into a complicated knot at the back of her head, and her pale skin was skillfully made up to give it color. Great care had been taken to accent a pair of greenish eyes. But it was her figure that impressed me most—sufficiently tall, well rounded, exactly what a woman's figure should be, except for her rather thick ankles and heavy legs. That made me feel better: I do have good legs.

The man beside her was big and blond and red-faced. Although he wore no coat or tie, he looked neither cool nor relaxed. His figure still revealed traces of leanness, but he was going to fat, especially around his middle.

"Miss Kincaid, I'd like you to meet my secretary, Nell Fincher, and her husband, B.J., my business manager."

"How do you do." Nell Fincher's manner was brisk yet friendly. Although she had hardly looked at me, I had the feeling she had registered everything, even counted the freckles across my nose. I caught a whiff of her perfume, spicy, like an exotic wood.

Her husband gave me a cool look, said hello and went directly to the bar at the end of the room. "Can I get anyone else a drink?"

Our host turned back to me and asked, "Wouldn't you like something stronger? No? I'll have one, B.J."

Although Mrs. Fincher said nothing, her husband set out three glasses and dropped ice into them.

"I nearly killed Miss Kincaid a few minutes ago—

ran my car into hers as I was going out the gate," Stansbury told the newcomers.

Mrs. Fincher was sitting in one of the heavy chairs that was included in the grouping around the sofa. Now she leaned forward and asked at once, "Were either of you injured?" Her voice was low and cool.

"I'm all right, but Miss Kincaid got a severe bump on her head."

"Hadn't I better call a doctor? You look a little shaken yourself, Elliott."

"I've already called Dr. Dorn. It's his day off, and his nurse is trying to find him."

"Is there anyone else you'd like me to call?" Nell asked me. "Family? Friends?" Her eyes were grayish green like the granite outcroppings along the river south of Bedford.

"Thank you, but there's no one to call. I just arrived in San Antonio yesterday afternoon, and I don't know anyone."

B.J. came up carrying all three glasses, grasping two of them in his huge right hand. As Elliott Stansbury took one, he explained, "Miss Kincaid came to San Antonio to find a job."

"Oh, and where is your home?" Nell Fincher accepted her drink from her husband without looking at him.

B.J. sank into the widest, softest chair in the group, flinging one leg across the other and sighing deeply. The drink he held was his second. I had seen him toss down the first one before preparing the others. He brushed a hand across his perspiring brow and wiped it on his trousers.

"I'm from Nebraska."

"What part?" B.J. asked, exhaling smoke from his thin cigar.

"South central. A little town called Bedford. We're only a few miles from the Kansas line."

"I went pheasant hunting in Franklin County, Nebraska, last fall. That anywhere near your town?" The words emerged from the left side of his mouth in almost a caustic snarl.

"Bedford is just in the next county."

"Terrific hunting in that country," he continued, sounding totally uninterested in the coincidence of its being so close to my home. "We got our limit every day. Stayed in Franklin, the only town in the county with a hotel or a motel. Is that anything like this place you come from?"

To my surprise, I rushed to Bedford's defense. "They're quite a bit alike. Bedford is a county seat, too. We've got a brand-new schoolhouse, a twenty-bed hospital, a small plastics firm, and the local farmers worth only a few hundred thousand dollars are considered small operators."

He remained unimpressed. "How come you didn't stay there and marry a big operator?"

"Because money doesn't interest me as much as a lot of other things," I snapped.

Nell Fincher broke in smoothly. "What made you decide to come to San Antonio?"

"I saw the Paseo del Rio on television one day and found it so fascinating that I went to the library and learned all I could about San Antonio. I liked the Spanish atmosphere, and the mild climate sounded great. Nebraska stays gray-brown from November until the middle of March. You can't imagine how cold it was when I left. It took me until this afternoon to thaw out. Your sunshine is heavenly."

"You think you'll like it here well enough to stay?" Nell asked, smiling.

The ice in B.J.'s drink clattered as he stared at me over the rim of his glass.

"I know I'm going to love it," I declared firmly.

"Wait until you've survived one of our summers," B.J. said sourly. "That TV story probably didn't tell you how hot they get."

"They can't be any worse than our Nebraska summers," I retorted.

Mr. Stansbury laughed. "I'm sure I don't have to tell you B.J. isn't a member of the chamber of commerce." B.J. wasn't a graduate of the Dale Carnegie course, either.

"It does seem odd that you chose San Antonio," Nell said. "I mean, most kids choose California or Florida or someplace where there's more excitement. I'm afraid you'll find San Antonio pretty dull." She sounded genial and friendly, but nothing about her ever seemed to warm up—not her eyes or her smile or her voice.

I shook my head. "I think San Antonio is exotic. I hear more Spanish than I do English; even the signs in the hotel garage are in both languages. At home everyone looks so much alike that their faces start to blur. Here I see black and brown faces as well as white ones. My eyes and ears can't keep up with all the sights and sounds."

B.J. got up abruptly and headed for the bar. The back of his shirt was damp with perspiration. "I'd think an accident within your first twenty-four hours would sour you on this town."

"If I'd ended up in the hospital seriously injured, it might have, but all I got was a bump on the head. Well, yes, I got something else, too," I amended. "The weirdest experience of my life. I saw a girl driving the car that hit me. I saw her as clearly as I'm seeing all of you now."

"A girl?" Nell Fincher's granite eyes began to glitter. They swept the two men's faces and came back to me. "That is weird. Raphaela and I are the only women in the house. Raphaela doesn't drive, and it wasn't I."

"No, it wasn't you. The girl was probably younger than I. She had long hair, dark blond, and she looked scared to death."

"Jeez, you did get a knock on the head, didn't you?" B.J. drawled, returning with his fresh drink.

"I saw her *before* the crash, not after."

"You mean you think you did."

They were all looking at me—Nell with those peculiar eyes, and B.J. with his hostile stare. On the wall beside the fireplace, the malevolent Sahara still threatened the kneeling Arab. Its menace seemed to have spilled out of the narrow black frame into the room. My scalp prickled, and I resolved to leave that house as quickly as I could.

The heavy silence was broken at that moment by Stansbury. Glancing at his watch, he said, "Nell, would you call John's office again? And if his nurse has left, try his house."

I set my iced tea down on the end table. "Mr. Stansbury, I really must be going." I tried to sound brisk and efficient. "If you'll just call me a cab, I'll get on back to my hotel."

"Please, I wouldn't sleep a wink tonight unless I

had John's word that you were all right." His soft, pink face was flooded with distress.

Nell, who had already risen, walked briskly from the room, her nylons whispering.

Stansbury turned to B.J. "Would you keep an eye out for the tow truck? I called a garage to come and get the cars. And the police should be here any minute, too. Take care of them."

"Sure." B.J. went to the bar and splashed some more bourbon over his ice before leaving.

Elliott Stansbury leaned forward and patted my arm. "I'm going to tell Raphaela that you're staying for dinner. I can't let you go back to your hotel until my doctor has assured me that you're all right."

"That's very kind of you, but I feel fine, really. I don't even have a headache anymore, and I'd like to get back to my hotel. If you'll just call a cab for me."

"But you're so alone! What if you suddenly became ill in the night? Please stay until John comes and has set my mind at rest. This is my first accident —thank God!—and it has upset me more than I can tell you."

His kindness and concern were so reassuring that despite B.J.'s offensive manner and his wife's serpentine coldness, I agreed to stay. That decision— although I didn't realize it at the time—marked the end of my "controlled environment," as Jack had called it, and landed me smack-dab in the middle of the real world.

"But as soon as your doctor has examined me," I said, "I'd like to go back to my hotel."

"And so you shall, my dear," he said earnestly. "I'm sorry you are in such a hurry to leave, but I realize that this has been a terrible experience for you. I'm most dreadfully sorry that I am to blame."

"You've been more than kind, and the experience hasn't been all that terrible. I seem to have made a bad impression on the Finchers, though."

Elliott Stansbury appeared nonplussed for a moment, and then he burst into laughter. "My dear young lady," he said, "you were complaining to me half an hour ago that people refuse to regard you as an adult. The Finchers are merely displaying the natural reserve adults show for one another when they meet for the first time." His eyes twinkled. "Welcome to adulthood."

I smiled back at him tentatively and wondered whether it was going to be all I had hoped it would be.

## CHAPTER TWO

Dinner was—well, interesting. The setting was sixteenth-century Spanish grandee: long refectory table of dark, almost black wood; heavy chairs with tall, carved backs and tapestry seats; a chandelier of several dozen electric candles that left the corners of the room shadowed. The food and conversation, however, were wholly contemporary. Nell, eyes glittering with excitement, described with heart-stopping detail her hobby, skydiving. B.J., who drank steadily through the meal—deliciously browned roast beef, fresh asparagus and apple crisp—took every opportunity to be abusive toward poor Raphaela, who served us. Then, apparently tired of that sport, he curtly interrupted his wife's conversation and began a long, rambling account of an elk-hunting trip he'd taken a few months earlier.

"B.J. does very well as long as he can keep both

feet on the ground, but he's terrified of flying." Nell's remark was tinged with contempt.

"So what? What's so challenging about flying?" he snarled. "Anyone can sit buckled into a seat or jump out of a plane and pull a rip cord. It takes stamina and brains to track an elk through the mountains and survive a sudden blizzard." He finished his drink abruptly and bellowed at Raphaela to bring him some brandy. The poor girl, who was serving coffee at the time, was so startled that she spilled it into my saucer.

Stansbury said quietly, "You may bring brandy for the ladies and myself, Raphaela. B.J. has had enough to drink. Please take the whiskey when you go out."

B.J.'s sweaty face turned an even deeper red. He avoided looking at any of us as he lit one of his little cigars, drawing on it heavily and exhaling with a rasping sound. He didn't say another word, but sat silently, sweating and smoking, while we had our brandy and coffee.

It was growing dark outside when Stansbury at last looked at his watch and said, "Nell, would you try once more to reach Dr. Dorn? Meanwhile, I'll show Miss Kincaid my garden."

As he led the way out of the dining room and into the foyer, he said, "If we can't get hold of Dr. Dorn, would you like me to try getting another doctor?"

"It won't be necessary. I'm feeling perfectly normal."

He nodded. "You've persuaded me. I watched you through dinner. If you noticed me staring at you, I must apologize, but you had me very worried, young lady." He stopped before the large glass doors and smiled at me. "No more hallucinations, no more girls smashing cars into you?"

"No," I said slowly. "It must have been the glare of the sun on your windshield. It's the only explanation that makes sense."

He nodded again, decisively. "I don't think we have to worry any longer about that bump on your head."

He opened the large glass doors, and we stepped out onto a flagstone portico that stood slightly above a huge formal courtyard. Just below our feet, a fountain was quietly chuckling. The water, which poured from a stone sculpture of a lion's head ran through an open duct to a pool of blue and yellow tiles in the center of the courtyard. Wide brick paths branched away from it, passing between tall palms that rose above the second-story windows to the open sky. There was nothing forbidding about the house seen from here. Although many of the first-floor rooms had been set back under arches to protect them from the direct rays of the sun, every room had windows opening onto the splendor of the courtyard. Some of the second-floor rooms had balconies with outside stairways. There was an air of oriental mystery and serenity about the place. All the loveliness of the house was concentrated here.

"It's beautiful," I exclaimed inadequately.

Elliott Stansbury smiled. "My flower garden is at the other end."

I followed him down the steps, past the gracefully curved pool, and finally into an elaborate garden. Here the brick paths narrowed and ran among the different flower beds. Over in one corner a gardener in orange coveralls was watering a flowering bush.

The roses—the only flower I could truly identify—were not yet in bloom, but there were others. Stansbury frequently stopped to touch a blossom lovingly and tell me its name. One fragrance, sweet and exotic, predominated over all the others. I discovered its source when we came upon a grouping of bushes and trellised vines covered with yellow and white blossoms.

"These are jasmine," Stansbury replied to my query.

"But the jasmine that I've seen everywhere down here doesn't have that fragrance," I remarked in surprise.

"You're speaking of the common yellow jasmine, *Jasminum fruiticans*. This is the common white jasmine, *Jasminum officinale*. It's a native of northern India and Persia, but it can be made to grow in any mild climate. You'll find it in southern Europe, too. This one happens to be the Spanish jasmine. Its branches are shorter, stouter, and if it is grafted to a two-year-old *Jasminum officinale*, it will grow into a bush that doesn't need any support."

There were other types of jasmine, too, some not yet blooming. He told me the botanical name of each one, but I didn't really care. I was entranced by that fragrance. It was enough to know that they were all jasmine. When we reached the corner where the gardener was watering, Stansbury said, "This is Raphaela's husband, Enrique."

He was young, slim, with a face like those I'd seen in photographs of Indians living high in the Andes—narrow, with high cheekbones and a finely sculptured nose. He acknowledged the introduction with grave courtesy, his dark eyes curious, searching.

"I suppose you could call me semiretired," my host explained as he led me down another path. "B.J. takes care of my oil and ranching interests. Nell, too. I never married, and they're a substitute for the family I never had. Nell's like a daughter to me, a very unusual woman. She's very intelligent and has a good head for business."

She's probably a lot smarter than her husband, I thought to myself, which gives him a very large pain in his male ego.

"I've had to find something to keep me busy," Stansbury went on. "I started with a dozen rose bushes, found I had a green thumb. . . ."

I lost the conclusion of his remark as something caught my eye. I had let my glance wander back to the sweet jasmine and was on the point of suggesting we go back there, when I saw a face in a second-story window. An inset balcony ran some twenty feet along the house at that particular point. Between the short supporting pillars I could see wide French doors. At each end of the balcony was a solid door leading into what I supposed were bedrooms. It was at the window of one of these rooms that I saw the girl's terrified face—the same face I had seen just before our cars crashed. Only this time there was a gag in the girl's mouth and even in that fading light I could see the terror in her expression. She weaved her head in an agonized effort to send me her message. She seemed unable to make any other movement, and I was certain her hands were bound behind her.

The face abruptly disappeared, and I tore my eyes away from the now-empty window, pretending to examine the blue and yellow tile mosaics on the nearby stretch of wall. I could hear the sound of

Elliott Stansbury's voice, but my mind couldn't grasp the meaning of his words. I knew now the menace I had sensed from the moment I saw the grim facade of this house. Whatever danger that girl was in, I had been sharing it every single moment since I regained consciousness in my crumpled car. One thought crowded everything else from my mind: I had to get away from this house as fast as possible.

The sound of Stansbury's voice stopped. I turned. He was looking at me as if he were waiting for some reply from me.

"Yes, you do have a beautiful garden," I declared.

I knew by the look on his face that my remark was a non sequitur. "Are you feeling all right?" he asked.

"I'm sorry. I'm afraid I was thinking about your lovely jasmine. Could we go back for a few moments? Then I really must leave."

"Of course." He led the way back to the jasmine, and I followed, my legs trembling. I wanted to cut and run, yet I dared not arouse his suspicions. When I left, he must be convinced that I knew nothing about the girl.

The girl! I almost groaned aloud. How could I ignore that silent, agonized look that pleaded for help with all the force of a scream? I couldn't ignore it. I had to do whatever I could to help her. A wave of revulsion swept over me as I watched Elliott Stansbury's slender body moving ahead of me on the brick path. Who was he? What corroding evil was hidden by his graciousness and charm? We reached the jasmine, and I buried my face in it, not wanting to look into his face or have him see mine. What was going on here? Why was he keeping that girl a prisoner in his house?

Again he said something I didn't hear. When I raised my head, he was regarding me strangely. "Are you sure you're all right?"

I started to reassure him and then leaped at the opportunity he had opened up. I hugged my bare arms and easily managed to shiver. "I'm fine, except that I'm a little chilly."

"I'm sorry. Come, we'll go back inside."

"I love it out here. If I could just have a sweater or some kind of wrap."

"Of course. I'm sure Nell has something you can wear. Enrique!" He turned to where the gardener had been standing as he watered the plants. But Enrique was gone. I had seen him leave moments before. "I'll get you something. I won't be a moment."

I waited until he had disappeared inside the house and then raced up the outside stairway that led to the balcony. I tried the knob of the door at the right end. It was locked, but I could see the knob moving, as if someone were trying to turn it from the inside. I waited, my breath coming in gasps, until it opened a crack. I pushed it open and burst inside. As I suspected, it was a small bedroom. The rumpled bed was covered with a striped, multicolored spread, and on one wall hung a gaudy painting of a bullfight. And there before me, her hands tied behind her back, another cord around her ankles, was the girl, sending me frantic messages with her eyes. How she was able to move about the room tied like that was a mystery. She was several years younger than I and rather plump. Her long blond hair was a mass of tangles, and two buttons had been ripped from her white blouse. Her flare-legged slacks were caught up in the cord that bound her ankles, revealing heavy platform shoes. The sole on her right shoe was at least two inches thicker than on the left one. Her brown eyes were wild with terror. I closed the door and ripped off the gag.

"I've been kidnapped," she gasped. "Please get me out of here." Her voice rose toward hysteria.

"I'll get you out of here," I quickly assured her, though at the moment I hadn't the faintest idea how. "Don't go to pieces. We don't want anyone to know that I'm up here."

"Call Daddy. Tell him to come and get me. They're going to do something to me. I can tell by the things they say to each other. I got away from them once. If I hadn't run into your car, I'd have escaped, but they caught me and dragged me back here."

"Are they all in it? The Finchers, too?"

"Yes, and the servants."

That meant I could look to no one else for help. I glanced out the window. The courtyard was empty. "I've only got five minutes at the most. Do you know where there's a phone?"

The girl shook her head. Tears were pouring down her face, but she was smothering her sobs.

"Don't worry, I'll find one," I told her. "I'll have to put the gag back on you in case somebody comes in."

She nodded, and I awkwardly replaced the gag with fingers that shook. "We'll have you out of here in no time," I promised and then went swiftly to the other door in the room. It opened onto a hallway. I decided the door to my left led into the French-doored room that opened onto the balcony. I tried it, found it unlocked and cautiously entered a large green and blue sitting room that smelled of cigar smoke. Yes, there was a phone on a table at one end of a sofa. With pounding heart I reached for it and then stopped. How did I ring the police? At home we had one emergency number, 2345, that you called in case of fire or if you wanted the sheriff or an ambulance. But here? The operator, of course. I dialed "0" with shaking fingers. "I need the police."

"Just a moment, I'll connect you." The line clicked, and I took a deep breath in an effort to steady my voice. When a man's voice answered, I said, "I want to report a kidnapping. There's a young girl out here who's being held a prisoner."

"What's the address?"

"I—I don't know, and I haven't time to look it up. Someone might come in at any minute. It's an estate; the owner's name is Elliott Stansbury. I was supposed to be on Mission Road, but I got lost and—— Oh, it's someplace in the south part of San Antonio, not too far inside the city limits."

"We can look up the address."

"Hurry!"

I hung up and ran back to the room where the girl was. She was sitting on the edge of the bed. Her eyes implored me as I entered. "I found a phone. The police will be here in a few minutes," I said as I moved swiftly to the window. If Elliott Stansbury had been there, I was prepared to hide for whatever time it took the police to arrive. But miraculously he had not yet returned with a sweater. "I'll have to go back down there so no one will suspect anything until the police get here." I went to her and laid a reassuring hand on her arm. "Don't worry anymore. This will be over in a few minutes."

She nodded, her eyes filled with tears. I returned to the garden as quickly as I could and sat down on a black iron bench beneath a palm tree. Only the rattle of the palm fronds high overhead and the thumping of my heart broke the silence. Stansbury returned a few moments later with a white sweater.

"I'm sorry I took so long, but I couldn't find Nell."

As he placed the soft sweater around my shoulders, I murmured a thank-you, hoping he wouldn't notice my breathlessness.

"Nell wasn't able to reach Dr. Dorn, unfortunately. I would so like to have had him examine you. Perhaps I should call someone else."

"There's really no need."

"You're sure you're all right? You aren't still seeing a girl at the wheel of my car?"

"No, I'm convinced I was mistaken."

"That's fine," he said with a relief that was not at all difficult for me to understand.

I was straining to pick up the sounds of sirens. Would the police never come? "It's so lovely out here," I said desperately, trying to fill in time. "You must enjoy your garden very much. Mother has some lilies and peonies, but she doesn't really care to garden." I went on discussing my mother's lack of a green thumb. Stansbury didn't seem to notice that I was babbling foolishly.

At last I heard them, far off. I buried my face in the jasmine. There would be no reason for him to believe they were coming here. But when it was apparent that they were coming up the driveway, Stansbury straightened and glanced toward the window where I had seen the girl, but he didn't move. Not I, however. I raced down the courtyard toward

the foyer, burst through the door and flung open the
front entrance. Two policemen stood there, guns
drawn, about to rush the door. Two more cars were
spilling out policemen, who were running about, taking positions. "I'm the one who phoned," I said
swiftly. "I'll show you where the girl is."

Three officers followed me as I ran back out into
the courtyard, past Elliott Stansbury, who exclaimed,
"What on earth!"

"She's in that room," I cried, pointing at the window. "Up those stairs."

The policemen brushed past me, one of them
advising, "You stay here, miss."

But I followed. They bounded up the steps two at
a time, and by the time I arrived at the top, they were
flinging open the unlocked door and rushing the
room. I heard a muttered oath and then nothing. I
stepped inside. The girl was gone.

## CHAPTER THREE

"What's the meaning of this?" Elliott Stansbury had come up the stairway and was standing in the doorway, a dumbfounded expression on his baby-pink face.

One of the policemen turned and, replacing his gun in its holster, said, "I'm Lieutenant Metcalf. We had a report that a girl had been kidnapped and was being held prisoner in this house."

"She *was* here," I insisted. I saw her and talked with her, and she asked me to help her."

Elliott Stansbury's dumbfounded expression faded. "Oh, I see," he said slowly. "Lieutenant, this girl was in an auto accident this afternoon and received a bump on her head. She's been acting strangely ever since."

"That's not true!" I protested. "I mean—I was in an accident, but there isn't a thing wrong with me.

The girl was here not half an hour ago." I poured out the whole story, about the accident, seeing the face at the window, talking to the girl after Elliott Stansbury had gone into the house to get a sweater for me. As I began my account, Nell and B.J. Fincher came out onto the balcony from their sitting room. Nell's green eyes were shining, and a strand of her auburn hair had fallen from the intricate knot at the back of her head and now drooped over her left temple. B.J. had changed into a fresh shirt and appeared cold sober.

When I finished my story, the lieutenant turned to the other policemen and said, "Search the house."

Nell spoke up in her low, pleasant voice, "I'll show them around, Elliott."

"This is my secretary, Mrs. Fincher."

The lieutenant nodded politely but said pointedly to his men, "Don't miss anything."

As his men followed Nell out of the small bedroom, I turned again to the lieutenant. "That's why he's kept me here as long as he could. He wanted to make sure before I left here that he'd convinced me I was mistaken about seeing the girl in the car. You wouldn't believe how charming he's been," I said, adding bitterly, "or how completely I was taken in." I glanced around the room uncertainly, trying to imagine how the girl could have been spirited away so quickly.

As we stood there waiting—B.J. smoking and sweating, pacing from the balcony into his sitting room and out again; Stansbury looking properly concerned about me; the lieutenant waiting, hard-eyed, watching all of us—the truth of the situation hit me. The click I'd heard on the telephone. I'd thought it was the operator, but someone in the house had been listening on an extension. They'd hurried and hidden the girl. That was why Stansbury had been so long getting the sweater. And they were able to hide her so well that Nell was confident enough to show them the house. I sat down abruptly on the rumpled bed. "They won't find her," I said glumly and explained.

Elliott Stansbury waited until I had finished and then shook his sleek white head regretfully. Another siren sounded, and he explained, replying to Lieutenant Metcalf's puzzled glance, "It's the ambulance I phoned for just before you arrived. She was behaving so irrationally." He sent me a pitying glance.

"I was not behaving irrationally!" I cried. He must have called the ambulance after he or someone else overheard me phoning the police. What better way to discredit my story! "Every word I've told you is true," I insisted to the lieutenant.

"We'll wait and see what my men find," he said so soothingly that my heart sank. It was obvious he thought there really was something wrong with me.

Raphaela entered the courtyard and looked up at the balcony. "It's the ambulance, Mr. Stansbury."

"Thank you, Raphaela."

Of course they didn't find the girl. She had been carefully hidden, undoubtedly by the Finchers while I waited below for the police to arrive. There was nothing more I could do for her. My immediate problem was all my own. I decided quickly that I'd be safer in a hospital than anywhere else for the time being. I let them lead me downstairs, where I lay down numbly on the ambulance cot and suffered the attendants to strap me down.

With Sir Laurence Olivier artistry, Elliott Stansbury bent over me, took my hand and said, "Don't be frightened. The doctors will take good care of you."

I couldn't tear my hand away because I was strapped down, and a choked cry of revulsion slipped past my clenched teeth. The kind, grandfatherly face slid from view as they rolled the cot into the ambulance. The doors banged closed, and I was driven away.

They took me to a hospital that, surprisingly, was located in downtown San Antonio. There I was X-rayed, had lights flashed in my eyes, my reflexes tested, and was finally put to bed. "You didn't find anything wrong with me, did you?" I asked the young doctor who had been in charge of me since I arrived.

"No, that blow to your head doesn't seem to have done any damage." His dark eyes continued to probe me, but his friendly smile relaxed his thin, tense face. "However, we'll keep you under observation overnight. If you still don't show any signs, we'll release you in the morning."

I wanted to tell him the real reason I was there and ask him for help, but I didn't dare. I couldn't risk his thinking that my problem was mental rather than physical. No, I wouldn't tell him my story and there was no use going back to the police in the morning, either. Perhaps the best thing I could do to help the girl was to keep quiet. Now that the kidnapping had been reported to the police—even if they didn't believe me—Elliott Stansbury and the Finchers wouldn't dare harm her. They would be prime suspects if she were found dead. I didn't see how they could just turn her loose, though. With her story backing up mine, they'd most certainly be arrested on a kidnapping charge.

Then, what could they do with her except kill her, making sure her body was never found? Even if she were reported missing, there would be no evidence against them. I hadn't been able to give the police a name, only a description, and my testimony was discredited now, even though the doctors failed to find anything wrong with me.

Recalling the girl's terror, I tossed and turned in frustration. Had I made things worse for her? Had I assured her death by calling the police and giving her kidnappers no other option? Murder! Dear God, what did I know about murder and murderers? Or even kidnappers? The only real-life murder I'd ever known about was a man in Bedford who'd been beaten to death one night on his back step while his wife and son slept in the house. His murderer was never found. I'd been too young at the time to be touched by the horror of it. Like the rest of the kids in town, I considered it simply a subject of great speculation and fascination.

I groaned and got out of bed, unable to lie still. I walked to the window and found myself to be four or five stories above the street. Traffic was light. I looked at my watch. It was 1:00 A.M. The blazing sign of the Hilton on the Paseo del Rio looked only a few blocks away, which meant my own hotel was close by. I recalled hearing ambulance sirens during the previous night. They must have been coming to this hospital. Somehow I felt better knowing I was back in familiar territory, as familiar as any place could be in a city where I was a stranger.

"There are germs out there. . . ." Jack's words came back to me, and I winced. I'd really muffed it. My first foray out of the controlled environment. How I'd been taken in by Elliott Stansbury's paternalism and charm! If only Jack were here now to tell me what to do; perhaps he could tell me what to do to help that poor girl—if only she was still alive.

"Oh, please let her be alive!" I whispered. "Please——"

Just then a grim, heavyset nurse came into the room and made me get back into bed. Then she ran another series of tests on my eyes and coordination to make sure, I suppose, that I wasn't suffering a delayed concussion or something. When she was finished, she said, "Now you must try to get some sleep. Are you in any pain?"

"No, I just can't sleep."

Her downy upper lip thrust itself thoughtfully over the lower. "You can't have a sedative, but the doctors said you could have some aspirin if you needed it. Let's try that. It helps some people relax and sleep."

So she brought the aspirin in a tiny paper cup. I downed it with some lukewarm water and, surprisingly, fell asleep.

The intense young doctor released me the next morning. When I went to the office to pay the bill, I was told that it had already been paid—by Elliott Stansbury. I walked out into warm sunlight and roaring traffic and headed for the Paseo del Rio. I took the first stairway I saw that went down to the river walk. The San Antonio River, which made a horseshoe bend through this section of the city, flowed as placidly as a canal along its cement banks, so calm that no current was visible. The water was brown but clear and no more than three or four feet deep. The tall old buildings that lined the banks faced the street above. Their lower floors, visible only from below, along the river, had for years been neglected, but now their basements were refurbished, their back doors gaily painted, and the space rented to cafés, bars, boutiques, and import shops. And everywhere there were trees and shrubs and flowers to revive the spirit and offer a blissful refuge from the jarring traffic of the city above. My own spirit, bruised by yesterday's events, began to heal as I gazed upon the serene loveliness of this unique sanctuary.

It was shortly before noon, and the walk on either side of the river was filled with strollers. The sidewalk cafés were already crowded with people having a leisurely drink or an early lunch. I had eaten very little of the bland hospital breakfast, and I was hungry. I stopped at a restaurant with a posted menu that featured lots of seafood, especially oysters. I sat down at a table in the sun, even though it hadn't been cleared yet, and scanned the newspaper someone had left behind. The paper didn't mention a word about the kidnapping, but that wasn't unusual. The victim's family was always warned not to contact the police. Somewhere in this city that girl's parents were suffering the most terrible anxiety while trying to get enough money together to meet the ransom. Or was the kidnapping an act of vengeance? If only I had asked the girl her father's name when she pleaded, "Call Daddy." My palms were sweating when I folded the paper so that the waitress could clear the table.

While waiting for my order, I looked through the help-wanted columns and found that secretaries and typists were in great demand. Well, that at least was comforting. One of the ads caught my eye immediately. "Just type accurately plus general office duties and go to work immediately." It sounded like something I could handle with no strain. I'd look for something more challenging after I got settled in. Despite the bizarre experiences that had greeted my arrival, I was staying. The sunshine, the serenity of the river and the fascination of this multicultured city far outweighed what had happened during the last twenty-four hours. I had wanted excitement and change, hadn't I? The fact that the city had offered me an overabundance of both did not diminish its charm for me.

The tables around me were filling up with businessmen and tourists. When there wasn't a morsel of French bread or a drop of Mornay sauce left, I leaned back to savor the last few swallows of the dark draft beer in my mug and to glance through the rest of the paper. And there she was. The photograph in the society section showed her smiling rather shyly. Laura Lynn Contreras, daughter of Mr. Faustino Contreras, was one of six young ladies invited by the Brackenridge Club to lead the debutante ball on Valentine's Day.

Faustino Contreras. The telephone book would give me his address. I jumped up so quickly that I knocked over the beer mug. Leaving the newspaper to absorb the mess, I hurried inside the café, where I was directed to a dark corner in the rear. After the brilliance of the sunshine, it took an agonizingly long time for my eyes to adjust to the dimness so that I could read the fine print in the directory. Faustino Contreras, 2201 Lamar Lynde Road. I paid the check and hurried to the street level, where I hailed a cab.

Lamar Lynde Road was in the northern part of San Antonio, an area of impressive homes, some of them walled estates that at one time were probably as isolated as Elliott Stansbury's. These places were now surrounded by newer homes, more practical in size and style. The cab turned down a shaded drive that led to a low, handsomely proportioned house of brown brick with cream-colored trim and ivy-covered walls. I paid the driver and rang the bell— three times. It was opened at last by a buxom Mexican woman whose carefully coiffured gray hair matched her silver-gray maid's uniform. When she saw me standing there, her eyes flickered unmistakably. "Yes, miss?"

"I'd like to see Mr. Contreras."

"Did you wish to see Mr. Faustino or Mr. Joseph Contreras?"

"Faustino Contreras, please."

For a moment she hesitated, then said stiffly, "Come in."

She led me from the marble-floored foyer into an enormous, yet cheerful, living room. Sunlight filtered through the many-paned windows from the front of the house. The furniture was casual, slip-covered in bright colors, with easy chairs drawn up on either side of a comfortable-looking couch. Bookshelves lined the wall behind it. It was a warm, inviting room.

"Have a chair, miss." She moved her hand toward the couch, "I'll tell Mr. Faustino you wish to see him."

I thanked her and sat down in the place she had indicated. But after five minutes I could sit still no longer and got up to wander about the room. I looked at the albums of rock music that lay haphazardly on a long stereo-TV console and noted that trade magazines from the oil industry greatly outnumbered the other publications that were arranged on the marble-topped coffee table. I recalled Elliott Stansbury's telling me of his oil and ranching interests. Above the fireplace was an enlarged colored photograph of a short, stocky man, a pretty blonde, blue-eyed woman, and two children. The handsome dark-haired boy looked about thirteen; the little girl, who was blonde, might have been ten years younger. It was a handsome family portrait, taken against a background of ivy and white latticework. The woman was seated in a rattan chair with a high fan back. The man was standing at her right with the boy in front of him and the little girl was at her left with her hand resting on her mother's knee. She could have been Laura Lynn.

I was still studying it when the man walked in. His face had lost all the youth that was so evident in the picture. Now it was a sad face with deep lines running from his nose to his mouth, which was stiffened with anger. Or was it pain? His black hair was streaked with gray. His immaculate white shirt made his brown skin appear even darker. He stood across the room from me in a sort of military posture, square-shouldered, yet with his thick, strong arms resting easily at his sides. I felt at once the extraordinary power that flowed from him. No wonder his daughter had cried, "Call Daddy." Faustino Contreras looked like a man who could handle anything.

"You wanted to see me?" he asked. His voice was deep and heavy.

"Mr. Contreras, I know where your daughter is," I said swiftly.

He stared at me; then his black eyes were shuttered. I suspected he didn't believe me, so I poured out my story in a breathless rush. "It was a stroke of luck that I saw her picture in this morning's paper and found out who she was. I took a cab out here as soon as I had looked up your address."

He stood there quietly; his expression was inscrutable. The only clue he gave that he had heard me was a flick of his fingers. "Miss . . . ?"

"Oh, I'm sorry. I'm Libby Kincaid."

"Well, Miss Kincaid, I appreciate your coming, and if the girl you saw had been my daughter, I'd be enormously grateful. But it couldn't have been she." His words were coldly polite, his tone impatient.

"But the picture in the paper? She was the girl I saw last night."

"My daughter is in her room at this moment, reading a book. Last night we were at home together watching TV."

Now it was my turn to stare. "But I saw her, your daughter, Laura Lynn, at Elliott Stansbury's house," I repeated slowly.

"She wasn't out of the house last night," he declared firmly. "Isabel popped some corn, and the three of us watched TV together. It happens to be one of our favorite ways to spend an evening."

A small knot of anger formed inside me. I said tartly, "Mr. Contreras, for the second time in twenty-four hours someone is trying to convince me that my eyes have deceived me. I let myself be persuaded of that once. But I'm not going to allow it to happen again."

The look on his face made my scalp prickle. What had I gotten myself into this time? He moved with barely controlled ferocity to the coffee table, where he took a cigarette from a carved wooden box. The lighter seemed to explode in his fingers. He exhaled the smoke slowly. When he finally spoke, his voice was harsh. "I don't know what your problem is, Miss Kincaid, but I warn you, don't involve my daughter. Now, I'd appreciate it if you'd leave."

Someone came in at that moment, and Faustino Contreras shot him a look of annoyance. It was the boy I had seen in the family photograph, now a young man. He had just come from a swim. He wore light-green bathing trunks and an open white beach jacket that exposed a measure of his smooth brown chest. He was not tall, scarcely medium height, but he had an athlete's body, lean and hard and well muscled. His dark hair was still damp but neatly combed. If he had noticed that he wasn't welcome, he gave no sign. His brown eyes examined me so boldly that I longed to freeze him with an icy look, but I couldn't manage it. Instead I flushed and looked away.

With only part of my attention, I heard Faustino

Contreras say, "This is my son, Joe. This is Miss Libby Kincaid. She is just leaving."

I snapped out of my haze. "Before I leave, I'd like to speak to your sister," I said addressing those brown eyes that continued their disturbing scrutiny.

"Are you a friend of Laura Lynn's?"

"Yes," I declared firmly, "and I think she's in trouble."

"Laura Lynn could only be in trouble with the library about overdue books. She spends too much time reading to get into any other kind."

"She wasn't reading yesterday afternoon when she crashed a car into mine when trying to escape from her kidnappers." I repeated the story to him while his father walked away from us and stood with his back to the room, smoking and gazing out the window.

"Miss Kincaid," Joe Contreras said when I had finished, "you've got to admit that's a pretty wild story." He was standing with his hands on his slim hips. A drop of water that his towel had missed lay in the hollow of his brown throat.

"If you think it sounds wild, you should have experienced it firsthand."

"Did this girl tell you her name was Laura Lynn Contreras?"

I replied acidly, "We didn't have time for a proper introduction."

"Well, whatever you experienced, Laura Lynn played no part in it."

"I suppose you were at home watching TV and eating popcorn with her, too!" I couldn't conceive of a more unlikely way for him to spend an evening.

There was a note of laughter in his voice as he replied, "Hardly."

"Which means that you don't know where your sister was last night."

"But I do, Miss Kincaid," Faustino Contreras broke in quickly, "and I can assure you that Laura Lynn is perfectly safe at this moment. And now, if you don't mind, I have some business to take care of."

"I'm not leaving here until I've seen her with my own eyes and know that she's as safe as you say."

He started for me. I think he was perfectly capable of grabbing my arms and forcibly putting me out of the house.

"Unless you let me see her, I'm going to the police," I gasped. It was an empty threat, my credibility with the police was minus zero after last night, and he should have known it. But it stopped him.

He looked angry enough to strangle me, but he said hoarsely, "All right." Then, turning on his heel, he stalked out of the room looking as dangerous as an enraged bear.

"What were you doing out at this Stansbury's house?" Joe Contreras asked. His glance had gone from warm to freezing.

"I was just driving by. I had been out looking for the old Spanish missions and got lost." Was Faustino Contreras really going after his daughter? *Maybe I should get out of here,* I thought. But no, I wanted to see whom they would produce.

"You're a tourist?" The drop of water at his throat dislodged and ran down his chest. He brushed it away absently.

"For a few days, perhaps, but then I intend to look for a job."

"I see." This bit of news didn't please him.

"If I survive these first few days," I added pointedly. "I've heard a lot about Texas hospitality. But I'm beginning to think I took the wrong fork in the road and ended up in Transylvania."

"I'm sorry if we appear unfriendly, but I can assure you there are no ghouls or mysteries here. I hope you'll be convinced of that when you see my sister."

"Perhaps. But even if she is here now, that doesn't mean that I didn't see her last night."

He shook his head. "Not Laura Lynn."

"She has long blond hair and brown eyes," I began determinedly.

"You could tell that from her picture."

"and one of her legs is shorter than the other— the right one I believe. She wears a built-up shoe on that foot."

His face darkened. "My sister has had enough pain in her young life. Neither you nor anyone else is going to hurt her anymore."

It sounded like a threat. "I don't want to hurt your sister. My God, I thought I was helping her. What——"

I didn't finish. Faustino Contreras returned, followed by the girl, alive and apparently free. She wore a sleeveless blouse and cut-offs and was barefoot. Her limp was pronounced. She looked pale and frightened, thinner than I remembered.

"Hello, Laura Lynn. Are you all right?"

"Of course. Why shouldn't I be?" She wouldn't look at me.

"Because the last time I saw you, you told me you'd been kidnapped and begged me to help you."

She shook her head, still not looking at me. "I've never seen you before in my life."

I had expected that. "Is this man really your father?"

She glanced up then. Was she startled or surprised? "Of course he's my father. Who do you think he is?"

"I don't know. But I do know there's something funny going on around here. If you need help, now's the time to speak up. You know you can trust me. I tried to help you once."

"As you can see, I don't need any help. But thank you for offering."

Her voice, warm, with a slight tremor, told me her thank-you was deeply felt. But it was clearly for services already rendered and no longer needed. She turned from me and walked out of the room. Her limp was noticeable but not unattractive.

"I've called a cab for you," her father said to me before he hurried to catch up with his daughter.

"Are you satisfied?" Joe Contreras asked, his dark eyes snapping with hostility.

"I'm not sure," I said slowly.

"Good Lord, what does it take to make you realize that Laura Lynn is OK, that she's alive and well in her own house? You might as well sit down and relax until the taxi gets here. There's no need for us to stand around like actors in some stupid TV drama."

I glanced around the room. If I sat in those deep armchairs, my legs would dangle ridiculously. I chose the edge of the couch, where I could sit with some grace. Ignoring the fact that his swimsuit was still damp, Joe Contreras flopped into an armchair, one brown leg thrown across the other, his bare foot bobbing. Refusing to be intimidated by his impatience, I declared firmly, "Laura Lynn was lying when she said she'd never seen me before. Why should she do that? Surely she—and the rest of you —know that I want to help her, that I would do her no harm."

"She wasn't lying," he said curtly. "She's never seen you before."

"You're wasting your breath," I said scornfully. "You people know as well as I do that Laura Lynn was a prisoner in Elliott Stansbury's house. Something weird is happening here. Give me one good reason why I shouldn't go to the police." I hoped the word *police* would jar him as much as it had his father.

He snorted. "Because I'll bet they've already got you pegged as a crazy."

"Maybe, but I'll bet they'd at least come out here and question you. That phony scene you just ran through won't fool them any more than it did me. Laura Lynn apparently can't lie as easily as you and your father."

He fixed me with his eyes as he spoke with a quiet intensity. "Look, if you really want to help Laura Lynn, don't go spreading this story to the police or anyone else."

I made no reply. After a long silence I turned my eyes away from his and searched for something else to fill them. I found the family portrait above the fireplace. "That doesn't look like Laura Lynn."

"It is."

"She isn't lame."

"Her leg was broken in an accident several years ago."

"Is that your mother?"

"Yes."

"Why wasn't she brought forward to try to convince me that Laura Lynn wasn't the girl I saw last night."

"She's dead."

"I'm sorry," I said quietly. "I thought—I mean, your father said Isabel popped corn and the three of them watched TV last night, and I——"

He cut short my embarrassed explanation. "Isabel is our maid."

"Oh, the woman who met me at the door. She seemed surprised to see me and no more pleased than the rest of you. Laura Lynn must have described me so well that Isabel recognized me. Probably something like 'She has long dark hair, blue eyes, and looks like a little girl.' Most people look at me and see a child."

"A child?" His eyes moved over me. "I wouldn't describe you that way at all."

It was a lovely compliment, even though I knew he didn't mean it as one. His tone was matter-of-fact, his eyes almost brutal. Suddenly I was so acutely aware of him I couldn't think of anything more to say. I rose and walked self-consciously to the window to watch for the cab. The house sat close to the ground, and just below the many-paned window, flowers were blooming, making a yellow and orange ruffle all around the front of the house. Through the wrought-iron fence, that enclosed the deep, sun-dappled lawn, I could see two small children riding their tricycles on the sidewalk.

Joe Contreras came up and stood behind me. "Have you found a place to live?"

"Not yet. I'm staying at La Mansion on the Paseo del Rio." The words were hardly out of my mouth before I regretted speaking them. I felt he had tricked me into telling him where I was living. That was something I didn't want him to know. "The taxi is coming." I felt immense relief as the cab nosed through one of the gates and headed toward the house. I started for the front door. Joe Contreras was walking beside me, his half-naked body moving as fluidly as if he were still in the water.

"What are you going to do?" he asked as he opened the door.

"I don't know," I replied and went out to the cab. As we drove away, I looked over my shoulder. Joe Contreras was standing in the open doorway staring after me. He was still there as we turned away from the gate.

## CHAPTER FOUR

As the cab made its way through the warm afternoon sunshine toward downtown San Antonio, I tried to make sense of the incidents that had crowded the past twenty-four hours. That Laura Lynn Contreras had been a prisoner in Elliott Stansbury's house was a fact, even though her father and brother and she herself, denied it. Of that I was certain. But how had she escaped? How did she get home? Why wasn't her kidnapping reported to the police? Why did all the Contrerases deny that there had been a kidnapping? Why did they want to keep it a secret? Faustino Contreras looked like a man who would kill anyone who dared touch a hair on his daughter's head.

That thought brought me up short. Perhaps that's what he was doing, going after those people himself rather than letting the law take over. On impulse I asked the cab driver, whose identification card gave his name as Carlos Martinez, if he knew Faustino Contreras.

The cabbie turned his face slightly toward me as he replied, "Yes, ma'am. That is, not personally, but he's one of the biggest wildcatters in the state. He's one big Chicano."

"I see. Do you know his daughter, Laura Lynn?"

"No, ma'am. You don't hear much about her. She was hurt in a plane crash a few years ago, the same one that killed her mother. It was a terrible thing. Faustino Contreras was piloting the plane." He kept his eyes on my image in his rearview mirror as he said, "Now, Joe Contreras, the son, he's something else! Everybody knows him." He clearly wanted to see how his words about Joe Contreras would affect me. As soon as he had maneuvered the cab around a huge truck, he again raised his eyes to the mirror to study my reflection. "That boy gets around."

A playboy, I thought disdainfully, with all the proper accouterments—good looks, money, self-assurance that bordered on arrogance. I felt my face heat up as I recalled my response to his physical presence.

"He doesn't play all the time, though," Martinez informed me. "Some people say he knows the wildcatting business as well as Faustino. He studied geology in college, and on top of that I hear he inherited his daddy's nose for oil."

"Wasn't he hurt in the plane crash?"

"He wasn't with them. A good thing, too, because Faustino was laid up in the hospital for quite a while afterward. Joe looked after the business." He fell silent for a moment, then shook his head. "They say Faustino Contreras hasn't been the same man since it happened."

No wonder Faustino Contreras's face looked so sad. And it was pain, then, that lurked around his mouth.

The sun was so hot that I rolled down the window and moved across the seat to the other side. Traffic was heavy. As we stopped for a light, a dark-blue Plymouth pulled up beside us. The driver, a man with dark hair graying at the temples, reminded me so much of my father that I felt a wave of homesickness. He must have sensed that I was staring at him, because he turned his head and looked at me. His face was thinner than my father's, his mouth less generous. I felt oddly disappointed. When the light changed, he pulled away quickly.

Suddenly I felt depressed; I couldn't bear the thought of returning to my lonely hotel room. "Isn't the zoo along here somewhere?"

"Yes, ma'am. The zoo and the sunken gardens. They're both up here in Brackenridge Park."

I knew that San Antonio was said to have a great zoo, one of the finest in the country, but I'd never heard of the sunken gardens.

"It was an old rock quarry," Martinez explained. "A few years ago the city decided to make something nice out of that big hole in the ground. It's best in the summer, when all the flowers are in bloom, but it's worth seeing anytime. It's only a little way from the zoo. I'd advise you to start with the gardens."

We had gone only three blocks when I saw the big sign for Brackenridge Park. The driver turned in and drove along the shaded lanes, past a colorful miniature train filled with sightseers. As we drove across a short bridge, he said, "This is an acequia. It's what's left of a huge canal network built by the missionaries so they could irrigate their fields with water from the river." He continued past the zoo entrance and guided the cab up an incline to a small parking area. "Just follow that path," he said. "It will take you up to the tea room and gardens."

I paid him and followed his directions. After a short walk I came to the tea room, which was housed in a small building. A sign in the window announced that it was closed. Nearby was a large open pavilion. Its roof was supported by thick pillars made of flat yellow stones piled one on top the other. This gave the pillars a scaly texture that I found repugnant. I walked over to the far side of the pavilion. There I could look down twenty or more feet into the bed of the old quarry. I saw shallow pools of sickly sepia-colored water, dotted with lily leaves, and paths that wound among barren flower beds, past obelisks, across small bridges made of the same scabrous yellow stone as the pavilion. The walls of the quarry were somewhat softened by some hardy trees and shrubs whose roots had somehow managed to penetrate the stubborn rocks. But there wasn't enough vegetation to counteract the heavy ocherous, atmosphere. I had to assume that when the flowers were in full bloom, the garden was transformed into a pleasant place, delightful to the eye. The thin waterfall on the left wall of the quarry was the only inducement to remain. It was almost hidden by a small glade of trees that shaded the path at that point. Except for a middle-aged Chinese couple, seated in the shade at the other end of the pavilion, the garden was deserted.

I made my way down the steps leading to the floor of the quarry. Here paths branched in several directions. I chose the one that led to the waterfall. The air was hot and still, and the glare of the water and stone made my eyes ache. I paused for a moment beside a bed of pansies, enjoying the smile on their bright, happy faces. Then, after crossing a stone bridge, I followed the path that led up a slight rise to the falls.

I sat down on a low stone wall that had been built along the cliff side of the path. From there I could watch the clear water spilling over the rocks as it rushed to the pool below. It was a quiet little haven, green and cool. The high cliff that sheltered it was heavily overgrown. In front of me the trees bordering the path cut off my view of the garden. On my right I could see a corner of the stone bridge I had just crossed; on my left was the path, which followed a winding course through more trees. The gentle splash of the waterfall and a few notes of bird song were the only sounds to be heard.

I leaned forward, chin on one hand, and closed my eyes. I couldn't recall ever feeling so weary. Of all the images that might have floated before my closed eyes, it was Joe Contreras whom I saw, brown and lean in his green swim trunks, the expression in his dark eyes ever-changing.

The sound of footsteps shattered my almost daydream. Coming up the path were two men dressed casually in slacks and sports shirts and wearing dark glasses. The one in the lead was tall and stocky, with red hair and a heavily freckled face. The other man was shorter and thick-chested. His Indian background was clearly evident from his high, prominent cheekbones and dark skin.

I drew my feet in so they could get by me on the narrow path, but instead of continuing their walk, they stopped. The tall one stood directly in front of me; the other man was a couple feet to my right.

"Libby Kincaid?" the burly one drawled.

Two days ago I'd have replied yes without hesitation. Now I surprised myself by saying coolly, "No, my name is Kathy Olson." It was the name of the girlfriend who had planned to come to San Antonio with me.

The man's arm shot out, pulling me up against him, one hand clamped over my mouth. "Very cute, but it won't work, baby doll. The only way you could ever disguise yourself would be to grow a few more inches. Hey, Paco, how many chicks do you know that are this small and still have all the right equipment?" He laughed.

I couldn't hear Paco's reply, but the arm around me moved higher, crushing my breasts. I gave a little cry of pain and nearly choked. The hand over my face was so big it was smothering me. I fought to be able to breathe, and mercifully my captor moved his hand enough to free my nose. I stopped struggling then; all I wanted was air. I breathed deeply, frantically.

"Whoever said good things come in small packages knew what he was talking about, eh, Paco?"

"Yeah, sure, Lonnie, but get on with it so we can get out of here."

"That's the trouble with you, Paco: you don't enjoy your work. Always in a hurry. Type A."

"Jesus, forget that lousy book you read, will you, and take care of the girl?"

"Sure, but don't say I didn't warn you when you wind up with a coronary."

"I'll have one right here if you don't get on with it."

The man called Lonnie tucked me under his arm. With his other hand still clamped on my mouth, he walked up the path to where there was a thin break in the trees that overlooked the pond. "You've been sticking your nose in other people's private business, and it's got you into a heap of trouble, baby doll. You've got a bad habit of going around telling everybody everything you know. The boss doesn't like it and wants it stopped. See that clump of water lilies out there? That's where you're going to land. I'm going to throw you down from here so you'll go splat against the bed of that pond. Too bad—but that's what happens to little girls who don't mind their own business."

Terror gave me strength. I twisted and kicked, but my struggles were as futile as those of a beetle between the fingers of a small boy.

"Sure seems like a waste, don't it, Paco, that we should be making garbage out of a good-looking chick like this? But we got our orders, don't we?"

"Yeah, sure." Paco's voice crackled with nervous tension.

" 'Course if you'd promise to leave town without saying another word, maybe I wouldn't have to do this to you."

I grew very still. It was the only way I could tell him that I agreed to his proposal.

He turned me around so that he could see my face. "You promise?"

I tried to nod. His huge hand was crushed against my head and mouth, making it impossible for me to speak.

His grin faded. "OK, baby doll, you got the message. Clear out of town, and don't come back. And keep your mouth shut. If the boss ever hears of you again, he'll track you down wherever you are and silence you for good." His hand slid down my body as he set me on the ground. "OK, Paco, let's go." They hurried down the path in the direction they had come from, with Lonnie in the lead.

I tottered over to the ledge by the waterfall and leaned heavily against the rough rock. My body ached like one big bruise; my lips felt raw, as if they were bleeding. It was my first experience with evil, and it had left me so shaken that I was afraid to move. It was some time before I could make my way down the path toward the pavilion. Upon seeing those scabrous rock pillars, I felt such a wave of nausea that I had to avert my eyes.

The Chinese couple were still there. I remember asking them about a phone and their shrugging and pointing down the road. Somehow I managed to keep on walking, past the closed café, across the parking lot, and down the road that led to the zoo. Partway there I found a phone booth. I dialed a cab company and asked them to send someone to pick me up; then I found a shady spot near the entrance gates and sat down on the grass, resting my head against the trunk of a tree. I was still trembling, but my mind was beginning to clear. I opened my purse and rummaged around for the card on which Elliott Stansbury had written the name and address of the garage that was repairing my car. I was going to pick it up, whether the dents had been hammered out or not, and drive to my hotel. Then I'd pack and be on my way. Where, I didn't know and didn't care. It didn't matter. I just wanted to get away from San Antonio, for good.

The taxi seemed to take much longer to arrive than the one that had picked me up at the Contreras home. After I told the driver the address of the garage, I sat back in my seat staring with unseeing eyes at the traffic and commercial buildings as they slid past the window.

My car was completely gutted. The mechanic told me it wouldn't be ready to drive, even if he didn't take time to fix the crushed fender and door, until Monday afternoon. Hearing the panic in my voice, he promised to try for Monday noon. There was nothing I could do. I called another cab and returned to my hotel.

I locked the door behind me and also the French doors that opened onto a narrow balcony shared with four other rooms. After that I settled myself comfortably on the bed with a sigh of relief. I felt safe for the moment.

Who wanted me out of San Antonio? Who sent those thugs after me? Who was "the boss"? Elliott Stansbury? Faustino Contreras? Both wanted to keep the kidnapping a secret. It was easy to understand why Elliott Stansbury would wish to do so. But Faustino Contreras?

I got up and went to the French doors. On the stone bridge that arched over the river below, a young couple stood with two small children. The man wore a cowboy hat and boots, the first man in ranch clothes I had seen in San Antonio. They looked like a happy family group. The girl held her mother's hand; the boy and his father, leaning over the parapet, were looking at something in the water below.

I turned away and paced back and forth in the narrow space between the bed and the heavily carved bureau. What good would it do if I figured out who had threatened my life? The only thing that mattered was getting out of town. Before we decided on San Antonio, Kathy and I had planned to go to New Orleans. I would go there. I could take a bus, but once I left San Antonio, I couldn't afford to come back to pick up my car. Elliott Stansbury knew that it was being repaired. He could find out easily enough when it would be ready. If it were Stansbury who wanted me out of town, he'd understand why I waited around until Monday afternoon. But Faustino Contreras wouldn't know. I decided to call him and tell him that because of my car, I couldn't leave San Antonio until Monday.

After I'd looked up the Contreras number, I sat staring at the phone. Then, having made up my mind, I dialed. I had expected that the maid would answer; instead I heard a voice that I recognized at once. "Hello. Joe Contreras speaking."

"This is Libby Kincaid," I stammered. "Tell your father my car had to be repaired and won't be finished until Monday afternoon. I'll pick it up then and leave town immediately." My hand shook as I put the phone back in its cradle.

## CHAPTER FIVE

I had dinner in the hotel that night and then went immediately back up to my room and locked myself in. The air conditioning was working only faintheartedly, and the room was warm, but no amount of discomfort could have induced me to open the balcony doors. I could find nothing on TV except crime shows, cops and robbers and lots of violence, which was not exactly what I needed to soothe my ragged nerves. I finally found an innocuous family comedy followed by an hourlong variety show.

I couldn't sleep that night. As soon as I started to doze off, I'd awaken with a violent jerk that left me shivering. Perhaps subconsciously I was afraid to go to sleep and dream. But how could my dreams have been any worse than my present situation? By morning I was groggy from the fatigue of two sleepless nights and two nightmare days. I showered and went downstairs for breakfast. I was surprised to find the coffee shop crowded at such an early hour on a Sunday morning. I found I wasn't hungry, but I ordered dry toast, orange juice and coffee and forced it down. I bought a paper and took it up to my room. There was nothing on TV but Sunday sermons. I chose one delivered by an earnest young man with a heavy Texas drawl.

I could hear people outdoors, calling to one another and laughing. I opened one of the French doors and went out on the balcony. The sun was bright and warm, and the world had that special Sunday look, relaxed and resting. A breeze rustled a crown of palm leaves on the far side of the balcony. Below the Paseo del Rio was filled with Sunday strollers. They looked so reassuringly and wholesomely normal that I felt my spirits lift.

A man and woman came out of the room on the right. They wished me good morning, set up a card table and dealt a hand of gin rummy. I felt self-conscious standing there a few feet away, although they seemed oblivious to my presence. Their easy companionship awakened a deep loneliness in me. I wandered back into my room and flipped through the paper again. I had left the TV on. The earnest young man had been replaced by a ranting old one.

It was eleven o'clock; I couldn't stand those four walls any longer. Before I was caught up in this incredible drama, I had planned to attend the mariachi mass at Mission San Jose. Now I asked myself what harm could come to me in a church. Both Elliott Stansbury and Faustino Contreras knew that I planned to leave town as soon as my car was repaired. I didn't know whether I was being watched or not. I had to assume I was. Well, what could be more innocent than going to church? After all I'd been through, who would deny me that?

The taxi deposited me at the wide gates set into the yellow stone walls enclosing the mission. I bought a ticket and entered the compound. It was very large; it must have covered several acres. At the far end, across a broad lawn, stood the magnificent old church. As I followed the path that led to it, I could see that small apartments, the quarters once occupied by the soldiers and Indians who lived at the mission, were built into the walls of the compound. In front of the apartments stood the old public ovens, shared by several families, who took turns cooking their food. The ovens, built from stones held together with mortar, looked like small igloos with short, square chimneys.

Because it was almost noon I got only one quick look at the magnificently carved entrance before I entered the chapel. It was already crowded, so I squeezed into a pew at the rear. The interior of the chapel was very plain. A single aisle led to a simple altar. Behind it, on a carved wooden panel, hung a slender, elegantly carved crucifix. The stark white walls were relieved only by an occasional sconce and small bas-relief sculptures of the stations of the cross.

Suddenly there was a blare of trumpets as the mariachi band entered the front of the church from an outside door at the right of the front pew. Looking solemn in their black suits with the short jackets and ruffled white shirts, they took their places before the altar rail. The voices of the choir, singing in Spanish, rose from the front of the church, too. I couldn't see them and wasn't sure whether they had been sitting there all the time or whether they had come in with the priest and the band. The music was stirring, joyous. I forgot all my troubles and fears as I witnessed this moving celebration of life and faith.

After the benediction, the congregation moved slowly toward the doors. I stood aside so that the others in the pew could step into the aisle and then sat down again to listen once more to the mariachi band, which showed no inclination to stop playing. When at last the music stopped, I made my way through the small group of people who lingered just inside the open door.

"Miss Kincaid!" I recognized the voice immediately and made for the door. A hand closed on my arm before I could escape. I tried to twist myself free, but Joe Contreras stood directly in my path. Breathlessly I exclaimed, "I can't leave before tomorrow afternoon. I saw no harm in attending church."

"I see no harm in it, either." His body was a barrier, so I stood before him, trembling.

People were jostling us as they left the church. Joe Contreras took my arm and led me across the grass, into the shade of a huisache tree. "I owe you an apology for my behavior yesterday and for my father's, too. We were not as civil as we should have been, considering that you had come there—I'm certain of it now—with the best intentions. We're both overly protective of Laura Lynn, and we react very strongly when we think she might be threatened."

"Thank you for your very understated apology." My voice was dry, but I was still trembling.

He looked at me queerly. "Now that you've met Laura Lynn, you can surely understand."

I plucked a huisache blossom from the branch over my head and examined it, maintaining my silence.

Joe Contreras said curtly, "I'm referring to her lameness, of course. It's hard for a teen-age girl."

The hint of anger in his tone sparked my smoldering rage. "Whatever Laura Lynn's problems may be, I don't think they justify sending two thugs to threaten my life if I don't leave San Antonio immediately and keep my mouth shut forever about what I've seen and heard!"

He stared at me. "Good God! Did someone do that?"

"The 'boss' sent them after me yesterday afternoon."

"The bastard!" he said harshly. "That's why you called last night. You thought it was Dad."

"Or Elliott Stansbury, I couldn't be sure which."

"I give you my word, neither Dad nor I had anything to do with that threat," he declared emphatically.

"Your word!" I exclaimed. "How can you ask me to take your word for anything after the lies your whole family told me yesterday?"

He reddened. "What I want you to understand," he said, groping for the right words, "is that there are limits to which Dad would go even to protect Laura Lynn."

"Can you be certain?" I demanded ruthlessly.

"Of course I'm certain," he snapped. My question had put him on the defensive. "I know Dad."

"Well, I don't, and I don't know you." As I turned and started away, he caught my arm. "Please, I"— he gestured helplessly with his other hand—"I wish you'd believe me. I'd like to help. I feel we owe you something——" He broke off and called, "Father, could I speak to you a moment?"

I glanced around and saw a brown-robed priest coming across the grass from the rear of the church. He was smiling, and when he reached us he shook Joe's hand warmly. "It's good to see you, Joe. How are your father and sister?" His features were honed by self-discipline. His eyes burned like blue fires far back beneath his white brows.

Joe Contreras hesitated, then replied, "They're fine, thank you. Father Donahue, this is Libby Kincaid. This young lady, for reasons I won't go into, believes I'm some sort of gangster. Would you give me a character reference?"

The burning eyes sparkled with mirth. I'm certain he thought this was a perfectly ordinary boy-girl dispute. "See that apartment over there, just to the right of that stone oven?" He pointed to one of the apartments built into the walls of the compound. In 1723 a young Indian girl who lived there with her parents married a Spanish soldier stationed at the Presidio de Bexar. His name was Jose Contreras. There have been Contrerases on the church records ever since, and please God there always will be. I wouldn't believe *everything* Joe tells you, of course. Joe winced visibly, and Father Donahue, after pausing and smiling mischievously, concluded, "But in important matters you can always trust him."

"I was hoping for an unqualified character reference," Joe said. "I'm afraid nothing less will do. Would you go so far as to tell her that she'd be perfectly safe to have lunch with me?"

"Without qualification." The priest nodded, smiling at both of us and left.

"Will you have lunch with me?" Joe asked.

I agreed rather stiffly, and we started for the gate in silence. But as we passed the apartment that the priest had indicated, my interest in the history of the mission overcame the antagonism I felt about Joe Contreras. "This is the first time I've seen the mission. I was on my way here Friday afternoon when I had the accident."

"Would you like me to show you around?" His tone was tentative, hopeful.

"I'd love it."

His self-assurance came flowing back, and he took my arm. "What better place to start than here in the two rooms where my ancestors lived?"

We stepped into a small room with whitewashed walls. It was empty now, except for the fireplace in one corner. "This, of course, was the kitchen, dining room, and living room. This," he said, going into the adjoining room, "was the bedroom." It, too, was small and contained the apartment's only window. "When my grandmother was alive, she used to go to mass with us. Afterward we'd stop here, and she'd tell me stories that had been handed down by *her* grandmother about life in the mission in its earliest years. I never wanted to leave, but Dad always broke it up saying we had to get home to dinner."

"I thought the living quarters within the walls here were for soldiers," I said.

"They did live here sometimes, but as a rule the army—although we wouldn't call it that today—the fifty to eighty soldiers who accompanied the priests, would build a fort or presidio a mile or two away from the mission. They were there to see that nothing happened to the monks while they converted the Indians to the Catholic faith and taught them Spanish. It was mostly the converts who lived within the walls and worked in the shops and the mill. There was a stone quarry, too, and, of course, farming. There were fields outside the compound where they raised cattle and grain. The friars built a remarkable irrigation system that brought water from the San Antonio River. At one time this mission had twelve hundred acres under irrigation and was running a herd of two hundred thousand Longhorns."

"And this was back in the 1700s?"

"From the mission's founding in 1720 to the end of the century."

I shook my head. "Where I come from, five hundred irrigated acres is a good-sized farm, and two hundred cows is a big herd."

"Well, there were about four hundred Indians living at the mission during that time."

He led me from the apartment back toward a large building that formed a corner of the compound. It was shaped like a Quonset hut. "This was the granary."

"It's hard to believe they could raise enough grain with their hand tools to fill this."

"Yes, it's remarkable." There was pride in his voice as he looked at the vast interior of the granary. "I'll show you the mill where they ground the grain."

He was an excellent guide, amusing, informative,

unabashedly proud that his roots went all the way back to the beginning of San Antonio's history. "It's all in there, the entire record of the mission," he said, indicating the library adjacent to the monastery, "including my family history."

When we were finally ready to leave, I stopped for one last look at the splendid old church. "It's so beautiful," I said quietly. "I can see why it's called Queen of the Missions."

Joe Contreras nodded and said, his voice warm with affection, "She's a grand old lady."

He took me to his car, and we drove into town. "I thought we might lunch on the Paseo del Rio. It's nice this time of year, when there aren't so many tourists."

We parked on the street across the river from my hotel and walked to the stairway at the end of the block. It was the hour of the promenade; it looked as if everybody in San Antonio and its environs were out on the streets. As we passed my hotel, I paused and pointed to a balcony on the third floor. "That's my room, the second from the corner."

"How did you happen to stay there?"

"I liked the description of it. You see, my girlfriend and I wrote for information about the city." I told him about Kathy and how, at the last moment, I had had to come alone. "I can't help thinking that if she'd come, I'd never have gotten mixed up in this crazy affair."

He made no comment, and we walked in silence for a few moments. At the foot of one of the arched bridges we were accosted by a tiny Mexican boy carrying a shoeshine kit. "Shoeshine, mister?" He was as aggressive as an insurance salesman, and his expression as hard-eyed as that of a loan officer. In fact, the only thing childlike about him was his size. Joe stopped. Placing his hand on top of the boy's head, he spoke to him in rapid Spanish. I was struck by the gentleness of the gesture, and I watched them both—Joe addressing the boy in Spanish, the boy replying firmly, decisively. At the end of the exchange, the boy knelt down and went to work on Joe's shoes.

"Do you know each other?" I asked.

Joe replied, "No. Juan says he began working the Paseo only last week. He works here nights and weekends."

"How old are you Juan?" I asked.

"Ten years old."

"Is business good?"

"Not yet, *señorita*, but it will get better," he answered without looking up.

The shine was completed with remarkable efficiency and speed. I decided he had evaluated his future business with the same cold-eyed realism with which he approached his customers.

We walked on a short distance to a café that exuded the spicy aroma of Mexican food. Joe led me firmly away from the two tables at the water's edge and chose one closer to the entrance. The space between the tables was throbbing with doves pecking away at crumbs. Once we were seated, I understood why Joe had chosen our table. The ones beside the river were shaded by a spreading magnolia tree. Perched on its branches among the shiny leaves was an enormous flock of doves. Between them and the diners below there seemed to be an uneasy truce.

The food was delicious, although it was seasoned with great restraint out of regard for the tourist palate. "Not like Isabel's, of course," Joe said. "I love Mexican food, but Dad always grouses when we have it. He doesn't like anything that reminds him of his Indian blood. As if by denying it himself, he could persuade others to forget it."

When I seemed surprised, he reminded me, "It isn't easy being a member of a minority anywhere in this country."

Flustered, I said, "I just didn't expect anything like that down here where there are as many people of Spanish extraction as Anglo-Saxon."

"A certain amount of prejudice exists, nevertheless. In social areas it's strong. Dad has spent most of his life trying to overcome it."

"And you?" I asked. He certainly didn't seem very defensive about it.

Joe grinned. "I'm a worse snob than the Anglos. I wouldn't trade my Indian-Spanish heritage for an ancestor who came over on the *Mayflower*." He grew serious. "It's different with Dad. He's never had the easy time of it that I've had. He had nothing when he started wildcatting for oil. It's a hard, brutal business. But through a combination of brains and luck, he made a lot of money by the time he was thirty. By then he'd met my mother. Her dad was a lieutenant colonel stationed here at Fort Sam before World War Two. He was overseas during the war when she and Dad got serious about each other. But she had promised her father she wouldn't get married until he came back. When he did, in 1945, he forbade her to marry Dad because he was a 'Mex' —that's what he called Dad. When Mother went ahead and got married anyway, her father disowned her. After he was transferred from Fort Sam, the only contact she had with her family was with one of her sisters. She never heard from the rest of her family again. Dad's always felt guilty about that, as if it were somehow his fault. Being a 'Mex' had never been easy, but this made it even harder for him. He can't understand how I can feel proud of my background and why I was always begging my grandmother to tell me stories about our family. He'd like to forget it all if he could."

We lingered over lunch until, finally, reluctantly, I said it was time I returned to my hotel.

"Look, if you haven't any plans for this afternoon, why not come out to my house for a swim?"

Although I wasn't looking forward to spending a long afternoon and evening in my hotel room, I said no. It came out too abruptly, but I had no desire to go back to that house.

He seemed to understand and added, "My father's at his office, and Laura Lynn is off someplace getting ready for the Debutante Ball. We'd have the house to ourselves. Isabel always goes to a matinee on Sunday afternoons."

"Thank you, but——"

"You still don't trust me," he said quietly.

It was an awkward moment, but I couldn't deny his statement. Whatever had become of that trusting kid whose brother, Jack, tried to warn her about the real world?

"Well, look, we don't have to go to my house. Would you like to see where the first Mrs. Jose

Contreras lived?" When I hesitated, he gestured down the river. "It's only a couple of blocks from here."

I agreed, relieved to put off the moment when I had to return to the loneliness and fear that waited for me in my hotel room.

We walked a short way beyond the Hilton Palacio del Rio and then up some steps to a quiet, little street paved with bricks. Small frame buildings lined either side of the street. "It's called La Villita, 'little village,' " Joe explained, "but you can see better what it's like from the next street." I followed as he led the way between two buildings. We came out into a walled village of ancient adobe houses. Their low roofs sloped down over wooden porches. Many of the buildings had been converted into shops. The house Joe led me to was one of the oldest and smallest.

"This isn't the actual house that the first Jose Contreras lived in, but it stood right on this spot. Originally this was an Indian village, but after the mission and presidio were built, it began to fill up with camp followers and tradesmen and soldiers' families. This is a restoration, but it's a living part of the city, as you can see. In addition to fostering the arts and crafts, it's used for a lot of social and cultural affairs. This city's attitude toward its Spanish blood is ambivalent—it treasures its Spanish history but can't seem to wholly accept contemporary Spanish culture."

He showed me more of that Spanish culture— past and present—that afternoon. We went to the Spanish governor's palace, which was converted from a presidio to the governor's residence when

San Antonio was made capital of the Spanish province of Texas. The long, narrow rooms with their beamed ceilings, stone floors and rough adobe walls surely must have seemed crude to the viceroy and his lady, who were accustomed to more elegant appointments.

From there it was a short walk to the Mexican business section, an area of narrow sidewalks and small shops. The air tingled with the smell of hot chilies. The open grocery stalls were filled with strange fruits and vegetables that Joe had to identify for me. Everywhere we went, people called greetings to him in Spanish.

I was astonished when he asked me to have dinner with him and saw, after consulting my watch, that it was six o'clock. "As you can see, you've been perfectly safe with me all afternoon," he said teasingly.

As a matter of fact, the hours I'd spent with Joe Contreras had pretty much done away with any remaining doubts I'd had about him. He had not offered in all that time any explanation of his family's efforts to keep Laura Lynn's kidnapping a secret. But whatever their reasons, I could no longer believe that the Contrerases meant me any harm. I was surprised to discover how much I had come to like Joe Contreras. Now, as I gazed at him and heard words echoing, "You've been perfectly safe with me all afternoon," I suspected that there was more behind those words than his teasing tone conveyed. I suspected that his motive in remaining at my side all afternoon had been to protect me. I should have been grateful—and I was—but I was also chagrined to realize that something more than my company had kept him there. It was that realization that made my acceptance sound somewhat less than enthusiastic.

"I've probably bored you this afternoon," he said stiffly. "I'm sorry. I——"

"But you haven't!" I broke in. "I enjoyed every moment! You've helped me through a very difficult day, and I can't tell you how grateful I am. But I think asking me to dinner is above and beyond the call of duty. You shouldn't feel any further responsibility for me, and if you'll take me back to my hotel, I can have dinner there. And I won't set foot outside until I go for my car in the morning."

"Whoa! I asked you to dinner, and I have no intention of backing down. Come on. Believe it or not, I know a very good restaurant that doesn't have a single Mexican dish on the menu."

It was indeed a very good restaurant. The quantity of crystal and silver on the table was slightly intimidating, but the service was so gracious, the food so delicious and Joe so amusing, that the dinner was a wholly delightful experience. I was sorry when it ended and we drove back to my hotel. Again Joe parked across the river from it, and we walked along the water's edge toward the hotel's river entrance. The crowds had gone; only an occasional couple passed us. From one of the bars down the river came the sound of a flamenco guitar, passionate, sad. When we came to a stone seat, Joe halted and said, "Sit down. There's something I'd like to tell you."

I sat down and waited. It was dark there, and I couldn't see his face clearly as he stood before me. "Four years ago," he began, "my father, mother and sister were flying down to Mexico. Dad has oil interests down there. He owns his own plane and flies down at least once a week. The plane crashed. My mother was killed, Laura Lynn and my father injured. Dad was out of the hospital in a couple of weeks, but Laura Lynn's leg was so badly broken that it took three operations to save it. In the end, it was several inches shorter than the other. Although the crash was caused by mechanical failure and not pilot error, Dad blames himself for my mother's death and for the ordeal Laura Lynn went through. Her lameness is a constant reminder, and he's always trying to make it up to her. Fortunately, the suffering Laura Lynn went through matured her beyond her years; she's unspoilable."

Someone walked by on the street above us. I could hear footsteps, smell the smoke of a cigarette. Behind Joe the river was lit by colored lights. Joe had his hands in his pockets, jingling some coins.

"Dad's got this obsession now about Laura Lynn being presented to San Antonio society. Mother was, in her day, and most of Laura Lynn's friends will be, and because of that Laura Lynn would like to be. But I don't think it would be a great disappointment to her if she weren't. It's Dad who's campaigned for it. He feels he owes it not only to Laura Lynn, but to Mother, to see that their daughter is accepted in the best social circles in spite of her Indian blood. It's all arranged. Laura Lynn has received her invitation to the Brackenridge Ball on February 14. Dad won't let anything prevent that no matter what he has to do. If the story of Laura Lynn's kidnapping were to be made public, there would be no Debutante Ball for her. That's all I can tell you, but it's necessary for you to know that much so you can understand why we lied to you yesterday."

I peered up at him, trying to read his face. "Why are you telling me this now?"

"Because, after spending the day with you, it's very important that you understand, at least partially, and not think too badly of me."

Somewhat breathlessly, I murmured, "I see."

He held out a hand to me and pulled me up gently into his arms. As he kissed me, I realized the day together had had an effect on me, too. A few spellbound moments later he asked, "Where will you go when you leave San Antonio?"

When I opened my eyes, I was, for some reason, surprised to see the colorfully lit river over Joe's shoulder. Thoroughly shaken, I replied in a voice that sounded like that of a stranger, "New Orleans."

"Will you call me as soon as you get there and let me know you're OK?"

"Yes."

Hand in hand we walked across the bridge and up the stairs of the river entrance to my hotel.

## CHAPTER SIX

I closed and locked the door, then walked slowly across the room to the long, low bureau. Switching on the lamp that stood on one end of it, I saw my face in the mirror. It occurred to me that it had been a long time since I had really looked at that face framed in long, dark hair worn plain and parted in the middle. I saw the turned-up nose that made my profile less than classic, the short, round chin. It was the eyes that surprised me. They weer almost those of a stranger. There was an expression in them I'd never seen before and couldn't for a moment identify. There was a darkness in them, a new depth that could be accounted for by the trauma of the last forty-eight hours. But there seemed to be more. I leaned closer. A woman's eyes looked back at me, not those of the girl everyone knew as Libby Kincaid. My cheeks flooded with color as I realized what —who— had brought about that change.

I opened the French doors and stepped out on the balcony. Below me was the stone bridge, and at the other end of it was the bench where I had sat listening while Joe told me about his mother's death and his father's consuming guilt. It was Joe's kiss that had changed the look in my eyes—probably forever.

As I gazed at the dark water reflecting the colored lights along the river banks and felt the soft night air on my face, I realized how much it was going to hurt to leave. San Antonio was a beautiful city, bright and warm. I had fallen in love with it at first sight. Now it had an even greater hold on my heart. Suddenly the colored lights blurred, but I reminded myself swiftly that Joe had asked me to call him when I reached New Orleans. Perhaps it would not end there.

I heard a sound behind me and whirled around. It was only the draperies blowing about in the breeze. But it was enough to revitalize the fear that I had managed to forget while I was with Joe. I left the balcony quickly, locking the doors behind me and pulling the heavy draperies closed.

After two nights of almost no sleep, I was exhausted. Following a warm bath, I fell asleep the moment my head touched the pillow. It was such a deep sleep that it took me a few moments to realize what was happening when two rough hands rolled me over and pressed my face into the pillow. As soon as I was fully awake, I began to struggle. The hands tightened cruelly, and Lonnie's voice rasped, "Take it easy, baby doll, or I'll put you back to sleep.

Paco! Don't just stand there. Tie her wrists and ankles."

Lonnie's huge hands immobilized me. It was like being pinned under an overturned truck. Even after I'd been trussed, with my wrists bound behind my back, he kept one hand on the back of my neck. I could scarcely breathe, and any attempt to scream brought on a smothering sensation.

"OK, baby doll, we're going to put a gag in your mouth, and if you try to scream, I'll kill you here and now, you hear?"

I nodded as best I could, and with unbelievable swiftness my face was turned on the pillow and a rag thrust into my mouth. Another rag was wrapped around it and knotted at the back of my head. Then Lonnie lifted me up and threw me over his shoulder. The French doors were open, and by the faint light that came through them I saw Lonnie's nervous friend, Paco, standing at the foot of the bed.

"Check the balcony," Lonnie ordered, and Paco moved to the open doors.

"It's clear," he said, "and there's nobody below."

So that's what they planned! I was to be thrown from my third-floor room to smash like a melon against the stone bridge! As Lonnie started toward the balcony I tried to throw myself from his shoulder, my throat straining to scream past the gag in my mouth. His hands gripped me harder; in my blind terror I struggled frantically against them. He went through the doors to the balcony, turned to the left and entered the open French doors of the adjoining room. I went limp, dizzy with relief and lack of air.

Lonnie understood. As he paused inside the room and waited for Paco to close both sets of doors, he said, chuckling, "So you thought I was going to throw you in the river? We can't do it that way, baby doll. You've already made yourself too well known to the police. The boss would be one of the first people they'd question when they found your body. We had to think of a better plan."

Except for the smell of cigarette smoke and a slightly rumpled bedspread, the room appeared uninhabited. Evidently they had rented it during the afternoon and waited there quietly until they felt it was safe to break into my room.

After Paco had closed the balcony doors, he went to the door to the hall. As he eased it open, a shaft of light touched the carpet. Because my head was hanging halfway down Lonnie's shoulder blade, I couldn't see Paco, but I heard him whisper, "It's OK. Come on."

Lonnie moved out into the corridor and walked quickly to the heavy door that led to the garage. The smell of gas fumes and rubber met my nostrils. They had parked their car in the space next to the door. Lonnie pulled me off his shoulder and laid me on the back seat. When he started to get in beside me, Paco said, "You drive, Lonnie."

A greasy strand of red hair had fallen across Lonnie's brow. He brushed it back with thick, freckled fingers as he announced in a tone of lip-smacking anticipation, "I'm riding back here with baby doll."

I could see both their faces now. My eyes flew to Paco, who was my only defense. His face might have been sculptured from wood; it was as hard and fierce as a ceremonial mask. "No, you drive, Lon. If you so much as touch that girl, I'm going to tell the boss. You know how he feels about things like that."

Lonnie glared at Paco. There was hatred in his narrow, lashless eyes, but after a moment he turned and went around the car to the driver's seat. Paco got in beside him, and the car moved down the winding ramp to the street.

Lonnie drove for fifteen or twenty minutes in total silence. But I knew he was quivering with rage. I was aware of it even through my terror. They meant to kill me. That was clear from the remarks Lonnie had made. But how? Where were they taking me? Who had ordered my execution hardly mattered. I recalled Joe's explaining his father's obsession with Laura Lynn's social debut. "Dad won't let anything prevent that," he had said, "no matter what he has to do." I was sure he hadn't realized all that statement conveyed. Joe had taken it for granted that his father would stop short of murder. I couldn't share his certainty. Faustino Contreras appeared as likely to want me dead as Elliott Stansbury.

At last the car slowed down. After a sharp turn, the sound of traffic faded in the distance. We drove along this quiet road for about five minutes and then turned again through a gate that I immediately recognized. For just an instant I felt a rush of sweet relief. This wasn't the Contreras house. Then the chilling reality of my predicament overwhelmed me, and silently I began to cry. The two solitary windows on the second floor were lighted and watched like baleful eyes as Lonnie lifted me from the seat and roughly slung me over his shoulder. The lights on the ground floor were hooded by the decorative arches around the windows, and it was so dark that Lonnie lost his footing and stumbled while crossing the flagstone porch. Paco opened the door for us, and the next moment I was staring down at the red-tiled floor of Elliott Stansbury's foyer. I heard him ask, "Did you have any trouble?"

"Are you kidding?" Lonnie exclaimed, indignant that anyone would suspect he'd bungle a job.

"Good. Take her upstairs, B.J."

B.J.'s feet and legs moved into view, and as I was transferred to his sweaty shoulder, I caught a glimpse of Elliott Stansbury standing gracefully at the foot of the stairway, one narrow hand on the banister, fully dressed in a silver-gray suit, black knitted tie, his white hair gleaming above his baby-pink face. I hadn't time to catch his expression, but his voice sounded as calm as if he were accepting the daily mail delivery,

Breathing much more heavily than my one hundred pounds warranted, B.J. carried me up the stairs. I was sobbing now, certain that death was only moments away. B.J. walked a short distance down a hall, into a brightly lighted room, where he dumped me carelessly on a bed. I landed on my back, so I was able to see at once that I was in the same bedroom that Laura Lynn Contreras had occupied. I recognized the gaudy bullfight print on the wall beside the bed, with its striped multicolored bedspread. As I turned my head to avoid the glare of the ceiling light, I saw B.J. standing beside the bed. He was regarding me with a triumphant expression, as if I were an elk he'd just shot. "Now you're going to get yours, little Miss Small Town." His lips formed an ugly curve.

Nell must have been waiting in the Finchers' sitting room, for she appeared immediately, wearing a sheer mint-green negligee over a matching nightgown. Her face was as carefully made up as if it were midday, but her chestnut hair hung long and loose about her soft, white throat. Excitement glittered like mica in her green, granitelike eyes. She gave me only a moment's glance. "Did everything go OK?"

"Yeah. No trouble at all, according to Lonnie."

They turned then and stepped aside to permit Elliott Stansbury to enter the room. "I sent the boys home," he told them. Gazing down at me, he said, "Well, Miss Kincaid, we meet again. It's unfortunate, but you wouldn't leave well enough alone, would you? You had to get involved with the Contrerases, and you ignored my warning to leave town."

With my eyes full of tears, I shook my head vigorously and tried to speak.

"Remove her gag, B.J.," he ordered. "There's no need to scream," he reminded me. "You know how isolated we are here."

As soon as the gag was pulled out of my mouth, I said, "I planned to leave at noon. I couldn't get my car——" But my tongue and throat were so dry that I began coughing and couldn't continue.

"My dear child," he said, incredulous, "we know all about your car, but how could you be so foolish as to wait for it once Lonnie and Paco had delivered my message? Have you never heard of buses? Is a car worth your life?"

He was right. What a stupid fool I'd been! I lay there silently, shivering in my pajamas.

"I'm sorry," he said with what sounded like genuine regret. "You leave me no alternative. You're so deeply involved now that I must have you killed. My business is much too lucrative to allow it to be exposed by a naïve little lady from Nebraska."

"After my calling the police out here the other night, you'll be the first person they suspect when they find me dead," I said hoarsely.

"But you are not going to be found—not ever. You'll be classified as a missing person, and that's what you'll remain. And after the way things turned out the other night, the police won't be surprised at all."

"They can check with the doctor at the hospital and find out there was nothing wrong with me."

"Perhaps nothing that showed on X rays, but you were acting peculiar, you know."

Raphaela appeared, looking sleepy but fully dressed in her black uniform with its white collar and cuffs. She glanced quickly at me and then as quickly away. Elliott Stansbury consulted his watch and said to her, "It's four o'clock. Nell will relieve you at eight so that you can fix breakfast. If she gives you any trouble at all, yell for B.J."

*Si, señor.*"

So I wasn't going to be killed immediately. I stopped shivering in the wake of the immense relief that swept me. Without giving me another glance, Elliott Stansbury and the Finchers went out. Raphaela carried the room's only chair, a rattan affair that appeared to be feather-light, across to the window. After she'd pulled back the short green curtains, she sat down and stared into the dark courtyard. I wondered what she could see out there; the window was a black mirror, reflecting the room and her face.

I shifted, trying to ease the ache in my arms and shoulders, and wriggled my fingers behind my back to get some blood flowing into them. I couldn't relate this room, plain and impersonal as a motel, to the rooms downstairs, where the furnishings were elaborate and oppressively heavy. Between the door and the bed was a spindly night table holding a green pottery lamp with a plastic shade. Across the room stood a small bureau, filmed with dust, the mirror above it streaked and dim. The brown tweed carpet looked almost brand-new. The sterility of the place precluded its being used as a guest room except for a very special type of guest—one like me. I wondered how many other victims, besides Laura Lynn Contreras and myself, had been prisoner here. Elliott Stansbury had discussed my impending death so casually that I was convinced there must have been others.

I started to shiver again. "I'm so cold," I said to Raphaela. "Would you cover me with the spread?"

She had started at the sound of my voice. Now she stared at me, her liquid dark eyes as frightened as those of a cornered animal.

"Please," I said. "You needn't worry. I'm as helpless as a baby."

She stood up and moved cautiously toward the bed. Her eyes swept over me, my thin pajamas covering my shaking body, my tightly bound ankles and wrists, and suddenly her wary expression changed. She looked upon me with undisguised pity. She pulled the bedspread down and from under my body with a certain gentleness and covered me with it.

"Thank you," I said as she straightened and stepped back.

"*De nada,*" she replied softly and went back to her chair.

Warmth began to spread through me almost immediately, and I was able to relax. I lay there watching Raphaela stare out into the night for a long time. Finally, because I wanted to think about something besides my death sentence, I asked, "How long have you been in this country?"

Again she started at the sound of my voice. Without looking at me she answered, "Two years, almost."

"Enrique, too?"

"*Sí.*"

"How long have you worked in this house?"

"The same."

"Do you like working here?"

For a moment I didn't think she was going to reply. After a long pause she said, "We were very poor in Mexico. Here we live in a nice house, earn much money and are never hungry. Someday we will have children and know that they, too, will never be hungry. If they get sick, we can take them to a doctor and buy medicine for them. They will go to school, and when they grow up they will be able to get good jobs and live well."

"Yes, of course." Although she couldn't have been more than five years older than I, she sounded old, joyless, squeezed out. "Do you have brothers and sisters?"

"I have four brothers and four sisters." The rattan chair creaked as she shifted in it. She still wouldn't look at me.

"Are any of the others here in the United States?"

"No, only me."

"You must get very lonely."

"I have Enrique," she said, her soft voice caressing his name.

"Of course, and I forgot that we're so close to Mexico down here. You can visit your family now and then."

"I cannot go back." It was said with a deep sadness that she evidently hadn't meant to reveal, for she stammered hastily, "I do not *want* to go back, that is what I meant to say. My English is not good," she added much too emphatically.

There was a pause, which I ended finally by saying, "I have an older brother, and right now I miss him very much."

"You don't have parents?" she asked stiffly.

"Yes. I miss them, too. They didn't want me to come to San Antonio. I wish I had listened to them."

"Yes, you should not have come."

I could think of nothing more to say. The room was silent until she looked over at me and asked, "Are you warm now?"

"Fine, thanks. Do you know when they're going to kill me?"

Her face twisted as if she were in great pain. "No," she whispered and looked down at her hands, which she kept clasping and unclasping in her lap.

"Well, at least it won't be until after they've had breakfast," I said, trying to keep my voice light.

Conversation was impossible for both of us after that. I'm not sure how much later it happened, but suddenly I fell asleep. Perhaps "lost consciousness" would be a better description. The strain of the past few days and the shock of knowing I was about to be killed were more than my system could tolerate, and the instinct for self-preservation permitted me to escape reality for a few hours.

Consciousness returned just as suddenly, as though someone had flipped a switch. I opened my eyes. Nell was standing at the window talking to B.J., who sat in the rattan chair. Raphaela had gone, I supposed, to prepare breakfast. The ceiling light had been turned off, and the bedroom was flooded with sunlight. I had no idea how long I'd slept. When I realized the Finchers were discussing me, I closed my eyes again and lay perfectly still.

"Elliott has already called Gomez," B.J. said, "and told him we're sending him the girl tonight to get rid of."

I peeped at them through my lashes. Although it couldn't have been later than midmorning, B.J. was drinking. A thick, squat glass, half full of whiskey, sat on the corner of the bureau. A full decanter stood beside it. A fresh shave had heightened the scalded look of B.J.'s face, which was damp with perspiration despite the cool air coming in through the open window.

But Nell appeared cool and composed. She was wearing a sleeveless dress, very nearly the color of her auburn hair. The straight, simple lines of the dress revealed her superb body—broad shoulders, narrow waist, full hips and breasts. She made an impatient gesture. "Gomez is stupid and lazy. He'll dig a grave two or three feet deep and call it a good job."

"Gomez is OK," B.J. said.

Nell shot him a contemptuous glance. "He's a bungler. If it hadn't been for him, the police wouldn't be watching Thompson; we wouldn't have had to kidnap the Contreras girl, and this whole thing never would have gotten started."

B.J.'s face turned an even deeper red under her scathing tone. "What the hell—you've enjoyed every minute of it. Who came up with the idea of kidnapping her? The closer you live to danger, the happier you are. You're nutty that way."

She smiled thinly. "If you think I'm going to defend myself because I'm not the vine-covered-cottage type with the bridge clubs and the kids, you're crazy. I'd rather be dead."

"Plenty of women seem to like it," B.J. said with a faint but unmistakable note of wistfulness in his voice.

"Well, I prefer excitement. And," she added pointedly with a glance at the glass on the bureau, "I can stand the pressure."

"Sure you can," he said bitterly. "You're a cold-blooded woman—the *coldest*."

She turned, catching his eyes and holding them as a smile touched her lips.

"Oh, hell," he said tiredly and looked away. "I didn't mean that way." He grabbed the glass and took a deep swallow. "And what difference will it make if Gomez digs her grave three feet deep or six? There are places in the Mexican desert that nobody sees for years at a time."

"I despise sloppy jobs, that's all." Her tone gave the impression that nothing better could be expected of B.J., either.

He took her jab sullenly. At that moment there was a knock on the open door, and Raphaela said, "Pardon. I have brought the girl's breakfast."

"Well, don't just stand there," B.J. snapped. "Bring it in. Set it on the bureau."

I made a big show of waking up. I straightened my cramped legs and groaned. They all glanced at me, but no one spoke to me directly.

"You want me to feed her?" Raphaela asked timidly.

"B.J. can feed her," Nell said.

"The hell I can! I'm no nursemaid. Let Raphaela do it."

Nell said, "Raphaela is supposed to serve my breakfast. It's your turn to guard her. Come on, Raphaela." Nell walked briskly across the room toward the door.

I broke in quickly before the women went out the door. "Would someone please take me to the bathroom?"

B.J. glared at the two women and exploded. "Now, by God, I'm not going to do that!"

Nell said, "Take her, Raphaela. I'll go on downstairs."

B.J. grabbed the bedspread, yanked it off me and pushed me over on my face, all his frustration and fury focusing on me. I felt a sharp tug at my wrists, then my ankles, and suddenly my arms and legs were free. "Get up," he ordered. "Follow Raphaela. I'll be right behind you, so don't try any tricks."

*As if I could,* I thought ruefully.

"This way," Raphaela said softly and started down the hall away from the Finchers' apartment. I followed, my legs as stiff as posts. I could hear B.J. breathing heavily behind me. Raphaela halted at the third door from my room, opened it and turned on the light. B.J. stopped a few feet away. He was obviously embarrassed, but there was no mistaking the menace in his voice as he reminded me, "Don't try anything funny."

I went in and closed the door. It was a good-sized bathroom, but like the bedroom where I was being kept, it had an unused look. The small yellow soap flowers in their brass dish looked dry and old. There was a trace of dust on the brown towels where they were folded over the brass bars. Before flushing the toilet, I eased open the medicine chest. It was empty.

"Hurry up!" The sharpness in B.J.'s tone carried through the bathroom door.

I flushed the toilet and opened the door with great reluctance. B.J. jerked a thumb back in the direction of my cell. "Get going." We returned the same way, with Raphaela in the lead, B.J. behind me. "On the bed," B.J. snarled. I lay down, and he bound my ankles once more, pulling the cord so tight that I protested.

"You're shutting off the blood."

"Shut up." He grabbed one of my arms and hauled me up to a sitting position on the edge of the bed. To Raphaela he snarled, "Put the tray beside her on the bed. She can feed herself."

Raphaela did as she was told, averting her eyes from me.

"Now, get out of here," B.J. told her, and she scurried away.

I drank the orange juice right down. I hadn't realized how thirsty I was. I gobbled up a slice of toast, but it made such a knot in my stomach that I couldn't swallow another bite. But I pretended to be hungry, spreading jam on the second slice, because I wanted to delay having my wrists bound again. I was uncomfortable enough, my legs throbbing and my feet numb.

B.J. sat across the room in the rattan chair, glowering at me. "Well, little Miss Small Town, how do you like San Antonio now?" he sneered.

"It's a beautiful city," I replied as I poured myself some coffee, "but I can't say as much for some of the people."

His laugh was ugly. "Say anything you want, kid. In a few more hours you'll be swallowing a mouthful of sand. Then you won't be smarting off." His eyes were small and mean. "Gomez has orders to kill you, but Elliott didn't say how or when. Gomez enjoys killing so much that he might not be in any hurry to get it over with." He grinned and said as an afterthought, "I'd sure like to be there. I've never seen a woman killed before."

*But I'll bet you've secretly wanted to kill one a thousand times,* I told him silently, thinking of Nell. Her sexual subjugation of him must be total and complete. I couldn't see him tolerating her scorn otherwise. The only outlet for his frustration seemed to be bullying any other woman who crossed his path.

"Think you're pretty cool, don't you?" he said, disappointed, I suppose, that I wasn't squirming under his calculated assault.

"I'm not dead yet," I reminded him and succeeded in bringing the coffee cup to my lips with a steady hand.

He was across the room in one stride, knocking the cup from my hand and jerking my legs up onto the bed, spilling the breakfast tray onto the floor. He yanked my arms behind my back and bound them as excruciatingly tight as he had my ankles. "No need to waste good food on you," he said, breathing heavily above me. "You're not going to need it."

Biting my lips against the pain, I heard him go to the balcony door and open it. A moment later Elliott Stansbury called up from the courtyard, "How is everything this morning?"

"OK," B.J. replied. "No trouble."

A few minutes later footsteps sounded on the cement steps leading up to the balcony, and Elliott Stansbury entered the room. He wore a sport shirt in beautifully variegated tones of cerise and burgundy and a pair of gray cotton trousers. In one hand he carried a pair of soiled gardening gloves, in the other a sprig of *Jasminum officinale,* which breathed its heavy fragrance into the room.

"Good morning, Miss Kincaid. Ah, I see you've had breakfast," he said, observing the debris of the tray lying on the floor.

"As much as B.J. thought I should have," I said.

"B.J. does have a tendency toward violence. I hope you're not too uncomfortable?"

"If these bonds aren't loosened, I'm going to have gangrene in my hands and feet."

"But we can't have you escaping. I wouldn't worry about the gangrene, my dear."

"Of course. What does it matter? You're soon going to kill me anyway and have me buried in the Mexican desert where I'll never be found."

"I see someone has been talking—B.J., I'll wager. I'm sorry, my dear. I'd prefer not to do this, but you give me no choice. Here, I've brought you something." He laid the sprig of jasmine near my face, touching the blossoms gently, caressing them. "I know how much you love it, and I'll make you a promise. I'll send a fresh sprig with you when you leave, with orders that it's to be placed on your grave." He smiled down at me. The naked evil in his smile, together with the cloying scent of the jasmine, brought on a sudden wave of nausea. I closed my eyes and swallowed the saliva that was pouring into my mouth. As if from a great distance his voice came to me, saying amiably, "I don't want you to think me completely heartless."

I turned my face away and, still desperately fighting nausea, I didn't hear him leave.

## CHAPTER SEVEN

After a while I felt better and blessedly alone in the room, with B.J. still out on the balcony. It was then that I was going to escape. I refused to lie there any longer, helplessly awaiting death.

There was no chance to escape as long as I was watched so closely, but as the morning wore on I found a ray of hope. B.J. obviously disliked the role of guard. If I gave him no reason to abuse me verbally or physically, he became bored and unable to sit still. He'd remain in the room, a few minutes, with the fragile rattan chair crackling under his restless, ponderous body; then he'd get up abruptly and move to the open balcony door. After leaning against the doorframe for a while, he'd finally go out onto the balcony. But that's as far as he went. The rattle of ice in his glass or the smell of his cigar told me he was nearby. His drinking or his boredom might give me a chance to run for it. But first I had to get loose from the cords that bound me. There was nothing in the bedroom I could use. I had searched the room half a dozen times, hoping to find something sharp enough to cut my bonds. And the bathroom was no more promising: not a sign of razor blade or scissors there.

Oh, for a knife! As the wish flashed through my mind, my eyes flew open. There had been a knife on my breakfast tray. True, it was only a table knife, but in the absence of any other tool it loomed in my mind as a treasure. Why hadn't I used my head during breakfast? I could have hidden the knife, could be using it right now, under the bedspread, to saw away at the cords. Beyond the edge of the bed I could see the corner of the breakfast tray that B.J. had overturned. The knife must be down there someplace. Cautiously I wriggled my body toward the edge of the bed. It couldn't be done quietly. The cheap mattress sounded as though it were stuffed with corn shucks. From the balcony came the clatter of ice cubes as if B.J. had suddenly pulled the glass away from his lips. I froze and waited, watching the doorway. After a moment I heard his lighter click and smelled fresh cigar smoke. I began inching toward the edge of the bed again.

At last I could see the debris that had been my breakfast—the insulated coffee server laying on its side, the slice of toast I'd spread jam on, the sticky plate, the tray lying facedown near the foot of the bed. I couldn't see the knife anywhere. The coffee cup had rolled across the floor and lay in front of the bureau. Had the knife, too, been sent flying when B.J. flung me back on the bed? My glance swept every inch of carpet visible from where I lay. The knife wasn't there. I hung my head over the side, hoping to lower it enough to see under the bed, when I saw the tip of the knife projecting just beyond the upside-down tray. I took a deep, trembling breath. How was I to get hold of it? Retrieving it with my mouth was out of the question Without my hands to hold me on the bed, I couldn't lower my head another inch without tumbling onto the floor. I lay back, resting and thinking. If I swung my feet to the floor and brought myself up to a sitting position, I could slide down onto the floor, then wriggle about until my fingers grasped the knife. I wasn't sure how I'd get back onto the bed, but I'd manage somehow if I could just get that knife!

Thrusting and twisting, I worked myself into a position that allowed my legs to stick out over the edge of the bed. Pushing against the mattress with one shoulder, I lunged upward but fell back. A second lunge brought me to a sitting position, and my legs dropped down. I sat there for a moment, trying to maintain my balance. My toes barely touched the floor.

"What the hell do you think you're doing?"

Like a puppet's, my head snapped around toward the balcony door. B.J. stood there staring at me, his empty glass and a cigar held in his left hand.

"I—I had to sit up," I stammered.

"Why?" He came into the room, glaring at me suspiciously.

"Because my shoulders ached from having my hands tied behind me." The ache was real enough, and it seemed at the moment a good reason to give.

It was an even better reason than I'd expected.

With a gleam of pleasure in his eyes, B.J. snarled, "Get those legs back up on the bed, kid, and if I catch you sitting up again, I'll lay you back down myself."

Wincing with pain, I lay down and pulled my legs back up onto the bed. Wanting to witness my discomfort a little longer, B.J. sank into the rattan chair and poured himself a fresh drink. I turned my back to him and lay, heart pounding, waiting for him to leave again.

But he showed no inclination to leave this time, and after half an hour or so I heard him snore. I ground my teeth in frustration. I couldn't risk resuming my efforts to get the knife. If he woke up and realized what I was doing, that would be the end of the knife. It would be the end of his carelessness, too. If he thought I was trying to escape, he'd never take his eyes off me again.

The minutes ticked by. I went over in my mind again and again the steps I would go through to get the knife. Each time, at the climactic moment, I could feel the cool metal of the knife in my fingers. I decided, too, that I could get myself back onto the bed by sitting on the floor, back against the edge of the bed, knees bent, and pushing with my feet and legs to lever myself up. All I needed was time and privacy, two elements most difficult to come by in my present situation.

I don't know how long B.J. slept, but finally I could stand it no longer. Every cell in my body was screaming for action. I faked a coughing spell, twisting about on the rustling matress as though fighting for breath. B.J., his big body slack in the chair, his chin on his chest, slept on undisturbed. With throat already burning, I put a bit more vigor into my coughs and suddenly choked. My paroxysms became the real thing, and I had to turn my face into the mattress to keep from strangling. When I finally found my breath, I lay there exhausted, eyes streaming with tears. As my vision cleared, I saw B.J. standing in the doorway to the balcony, a fresh drink in his hand, exhaling slowly the smoke from a newly lit cigar. His back was to the room. There was no doubt that his disinterest in me was genuine and total.

I had to wait only a few minutes before he moved out on the balcony. The rustling of the mattress this time must have appeared entirely innocent to him. He remained outside. My initial effort to sit up once I reached the edge of the bed failed, and I was about to make a second try when Raphaela walked in. She looked startled, and she realized what I was trying to do. When her eyes probed the room swiftly and she asked, "Where is *Señor* Fincher?" I breathed easier.

"On the balcony," I replied.

Hearing our voices, he appeared in the doorway. "It's about time," he muttered and started into the room.

Raphaela spoke quickly. "I have come to collect the breakfast tray. I must wash the dishes. I will be back as soon as I have finished."

"Well, hurry up, you hear?"

B.J. went back onto the balcony, and Raphaela knelt to pick up the litter of my aborted breakfast. In a desperate attempt to distract her so that she would overlook the knife, I said, "I didn't make that mess. B.J. got mad at me. He knocked the coffee cup out of my hands and upset the tray in the bargain. He said there was no sense in feeding me, since I'd soon be dead."

"That is the kind of thing he would do," she whispered, and there was naked hatred in her voice. "He is a very angry man always." Onto the tray went the coffee server and plate.

"It's plain to see why," I said. The toast and napkin were retrieved.

"Yes, *Señora* Fincher does not love him. I think she cannot love anyone." Her fingers grasped the sticky knife firmly and tossed it in the tray.

"I think you're right," I agreed in a small voice.

She gathered up the coffee cup and went out, carrying the tray and my best hope for escape.

Raphaela brought my lunch when she arrived an hour later to relieve B.J. There was a plastic glass of iced tea and a tuna-fish sandwich. No silverware. B.J. untied my hands, and then, to make sure Raphaela could retie me properly, he showed her how and had her repeat the operation a few times. When he was convinced that she could bind me so that I couldn't get loose, he left to eat his own lunch.

The iced tea I drank thirstily. The tuna-fish sandwich I could barely tolerate, but I ate it doggedly, bite by bite, washing it down with the tea. I took my time, relishing the temporary release from my bonds. When I couldn't put off eating the last bite any longer, Raphaela left her chair by the window and retied my wrists snugly and competently, though not as painfully tight as B.J. had. She returned to her chair, and I to my escape plan.

Time was running out. A few more hours and

I'd be on my way to Mexico. The sinking feeling this thought aroused was so powerful that it shut off all my mental processes for a few minutes. When I was back in control, I strained against my bonds, testing them. Cutting myself loose was now out of the question. My only recourse was to work free. But it was immediately obvious that the way I was tied at the moment made this impossible. The cords around my ankles, which B.J. had knotted, were torturously tight. It would be futile to spend any time or effort straining against them. I turned my back to the wall, my face to Raphaela, and began working on my wrist bindings. I had some play in my wrists and quite a lot in my fingers.

After half an hour or so I was exhausted, and my wrists felt as if someone had run them through a wringer. As I lay there resting, my body prickling with sweat, once more I had to fight against despair. The thought of Joe proved to be my weapon. Last night I hadn't permitted myself to get too specific about what I felt for him. Now I unabashedly admitted to myself that I was in love with him. I really couldn't believe he was in love with me, but he *had* asked me to call him when I reached New Orleans. It was something to build on, provided I was given time. And since no one was inclined to grant me that time, I'd have to win it through my own efforts. Once again I began forcing my bruised wrists against their bonds.

When fatigue and the pain in my wrists forced me to rest a second time, I couldn't see that I had made progress at all. Raphaela had avoided looking at me since she had tied my wrists after lunch. I could almost feel her tension.

"They're sending me to Mexico to someone named Gomez. Do you know him?" I asked.

She jumped as I broke the silence. Looking down at her hands twisting in her lap, she said, "I have never met him, but I have heard *Señor* Stansbury speak of him."

I bore down on her hard. "He's to bury me out in the desert someplace where my body won't be found."

"Please do not talk about it!" she cried.

"If I can speak of it, surely you can listen."

Her liquid brown eyes were beseeching. "You must understand that I would not help *Señor* Stansbury with this if I did not have to."

"I don't know what reasons you have for helping him, Raphaela, but surely they aren't so important that you'd help him kill me."

"Please!" she cried again, covering her ears. She looked away and stared determinedly out the window.

I lay quietly and waited. After she had cautiously removed her hands from her ears, I began again. "You're the only one who can help me, Raphaela. You're the only one who doesn't want to see me dead. If you'd untie my hands and leave the room for only five minutes, I could get away."

She shook her head and moaned, "I cannot."

"No one need know that you untied me. They'll think I worked loose by myself."

"It would not matter. They would blame me anyway and——" She broke off, and once again her hands began working in her lap.

"And they would kill you, too," I finished for her.

"No," she said bitterly. *"Señor* Stansbury wouldn't

have to kill me. He would only have to call the immigration authorities and tell them I am here illegally. I would be sent back to Mexico. I would lose Enrique. He has told me I must do whatever *Señor* Stansbury wishes me to. He will do anything to stay here. I would rather die than lose Enrique."

My heart sank. Her love for Enrique was stronger than any repugnance she felt about helping with my murder. Well, it had been worth a try, anyhow.

I went back to the only course of action available to me. It was fortunate that Raphaela wouldn't look at me. As I worked my wrists, I could no longer keep from grimacing with pain. During one of my rest periods, I asked to be taken to the bathroom. She refused at first, clearly suspicious that I was up to something. I wasn't. I merely wanted to go to the bathroom.

"Please, Raphaela. I promise I won't try to escape."

She hesitated, then came reluctantly over to the bed and threw back the spread. "I will untie your feet this time, but not your hands." As she pushed up the legs of my pajamas to get at the ropes, I heard her draw in her breath sharply. Evidently my legs looked as bad as they felt. I stumbled as I took the first few steps down the hall with Raphaela following right behind me. She came into the bathroom with me, helping me with my pajamas and remaining with me until I had finished. The walk back to the bedroom, with her hand on one of my arms, was brisk. She retied my ankles swiftly and with an unmistakable air of relief. After pulling the spread up over me, she returned to her chair and began worrying a loose fiber on one of its arms.

"What time is it?" I asked.

She looked at the round, inexpensive watch on her arm and replied, "Four o'clock."

"How much more time do I have?"

The fear of losing Enrique, reawakened by my attempts to persuade her to help me escape, was like armor plate. My question touched neither her conscience nor her pity. "I do not know," she said indifferently.

Suddenly I felt terribly lonely. I hadn't realized how much support her compassion had provided until it was withdrawn. For some strange reason I had felt closer to her than anyone I'd met since coming to San Antonio, except for Joe. At the thought of Joe, my throat tightened, and I squirmed over onto my back, too miserable to lie still. If only——

My thoughts broke off sharply as I realized I had more movement in my ankles than at any time since I'd been bound. I twisted them cautiously to confirm my first impression and then lay still, heart pounding. Whether through carelessness or through pity because of what the cords had done to my legs, Raphaela had retied me rather loosely. Maybe, just maybe, I could work my legs free.

"What is wrong?" Raphaela's voice cut through my intense concentration on my ankles.

I lay perfectly still. She came over to the bed. "Are you all right?"

I looked up at her and said, "It's just that my feet are so cold. I can make them a little warmer by rubbing them against the blankets."

Her eyes moved down my covered form to my feet and paused there a few moments. Then, apparently accepting my explanation, she pulled the blanket up over my feet and returned to her post by the window.

As I carefully continued my efforts to work my feet free of my bonds, I considered what I would do if I succeeded. Escape while Raphaela was on guard was impossible. She performed her duty too conscientiously. The only opportunity I would have to make my move would be while B.J. was watching me, during one of those moments when his restlessness had driven him out to the balcony. Or perhaps he would fall asleep again. Suddenly I recalled how profoundly I had slept that morning. B.J. and Nell had been witness to that. Perhaps if I faked another nap, B.J. would drop his guard sufficiently to give me a good chance to escape.

"What time will you have to leave to prepare dinner?" I asked Raphaela.

She turned her head toward me, her expression suspicious. "Why do you wish to know?"

"Because," I said firmly, "I don't like to be guarded by B.J. I dread the thought of his coming back."

She looked again at her watch. "*Señor* Stansbury told me to plan a dinner that could be prepared in a short time. B.J. will not be here until six o'clock."

There wasn't much time, then. Once B.J. arrived my efforts to work free would have to be curtailed, perhaps abandoned. He was likely to suspect the real reason I was twisting my feet. I had to work them loose before then.

I put a little more force behind my twistings and turnings, biting my lips against the pain and trying to keep my breathing normal. I was making some headway, I could tell, but it was maddeningly slow.

I wasn't even certain at first that my right foot had pulled free, because from the knee down my leg was a mass of throbbing pain. But a tentative upward movement indicated that it was indeed free. I let the leg drop back slowly and lay there, eyes squeezed shut, forcing myself to breathe slowly, my pulse pounding in my throat. As I lay there, resting, I heard B.J. come in and ask, "Is she asleep?"

"Yes, she fell asleep a few minutes ago."

"Call me when dinner is ready. If she's still asleep, I'll come down and eat with Elliott and my wife."

"Yes, *señor*."

I heard the clink of glass, the sloshing of liquid being poured. No need to risk opening my eyes a crack to know that B.J. had brought his decanter and glass along to keep him company. It was hard lying perfectly still while every nerve in my body was jumping. Once, unable to bear it any longer, I groaned faintly and tossed about, then subsided into a deep pretend sleep once more.

"*Señor*." It was Raphaela down in the courtyard.

"Yeah?"

"Dinner is ready to be served."

There was a pause. I didn't risk peeping between my lids. B.J. moved over to the bed. I could hear him breathing above me, so close I could feel the heat of his body. I lay very still. Convinced that I was asleep and that I'd remain in that state for a while, he left the room. I heard his footsteps fade down the hall. Still I lay there. When I was sure he was gone, I cautiously shook my left ankle free of the rope and scooted to the edge of the bed. Swinging my feet to the floor, I struggled to bring my body to a sitting position. From there it was easy. My eyes had searched the room dozens of times. I knew there was nothing in it I could use to cut the rope around my wrists, and running would be difficult with my arms bound behind my back. But for the moment, cutting my arms free was less important than getting out of that room.

B.J. had left the door open behind him, but I decided the best escape route was through the courtyard and out a back gate. I hadn't seen a back gate, but there had to be some way out of the courtyard. I went swiftly to the balcony door, backed up to it and twisted the knob. It came open with a click. I waited for a moment, then dashed out the door and down the steps.

At that hour the courtyard was not yet entirely dark, and it was lit by lights shinning from various windows. I ran toward the garden, sweeping the rear area with my eyes, searching for an exit. There didn't seem to be any. There was no gate, only doors. Doors opening into rooms. I ran, footsteps padding on the brick walk, the smell of jasmine now sickeningly strong. I hurried past the flowers, then stopped, remembering that one bush had been trained to a metal trellis.

I turned and retraced my steps. I found a sharp end on one of the metal bars, backed up to it and began sawing awkwardly. The heavy scent from the bush filled my nose. That fragrance, once so sweet to me, now represented horror and evil. I never wanted to smell jasmine again as long as I lived.

At last my wrists were free. By that time I knew where I was going. Through one of the lighted windows at the back I could see Raphaela moving back and forth in what was obviously the kitchen. I made for it, crouching at the edge of the garden behind a bush while I watched. Sooner or later she'd have to go from the kitchen to the dining room. As soon as she left, I meant to dash through the kitchen and out the side door, which I could see through the window. I was certain that it led outside the house. I waited, shivering from the chill of the evening air and the tension.

When Raphaela finally left the room, I dashed into the empty kitchen and without pausing for breath, sped toward the outside door. I was only halfway across the room when Raphaela walked through the swinging door between the kitchen and the dining room. I skidded to a stop, and Raphaela froze. The only sound was the whisper of the swinging door as it settled back into place. Raphaela stared at me, her eyes wide, her mouth forming a cry of alarm.

## CHAPTER EIGHT

I stared back, waiting for the scream that would shatter my hope of escaping. When it didn't come, I was freed from my paralysis. I ran for the door. Just before I went through it, I looked back at Raphaela. She hadn't moved, but she'd closed her mouth and was watching me, her brown face a sickly yellow. Suddenly her eyes flew to the door I had just come through. Enrique came in, brushing his hands on his orange coveralls, blinking in the strong light. There was no lag between his sighting me and his response. He yelled. As I shot out the door, Raphaela joined her husband in giving the alarm.

I plunged through the gathering darkness across the rear lawn toward the impenetrable bamboo hedge that enclosed the estate. Somewhere there had to be a gate. Yes, there it was—a heavy wooden gate painted green. Struggling with the tight latch, I

heard footsteps pounding behind me and the sound
of angry, excited voices. Over my shoulder as I
darted through the gate, I saw a flash of orange.
Enrique was pursuing me. I set myself a straight path
toward a grove of trees some eighty feet away and
ran for my life.

The ground was rough and sparsely covered with
wild grasses. Each pounding step sent pain shooting
from my bare feet to my knees, but nothing could
have slowed me down.

"Get the hell out of the way, Hank," B.J. shouted,
and almost at the same moment came the sound of
a shot and the whine of a bullet over my head. I
darted to my right, and the next bullet, low enough
this time, went past me on the left. As I continued
to zigzag, I was able to see what was going on behind
me. Enrique had moved to the right to get out of the
way of the gun. While I zigzagged, he followed a
straight course and was gaining on me. B.J., slowed
by his bulk, was far behind. But this disadvantage
was more than made up for by his gun. Another
shot whined past me as a stitch in my side grabbed
me so that I stumbled, gasping with pain. I forced
myself to continue until I had covered the last
few yards that led into a grove of trees.

The trees were small, probably not more than
twelve or fifteen feet high, the trunks smaller around
than my arm, standing as thickly as if they'd been
sown like oats. It was impossible to run through
them. I lurched about, following a twisting, turning
course that soon had me sobbing in frustration.
Enrique was still pursuing me, threading his way
through the trees just as I was doing. My glance fell
on him just as he careened into a tree with such

impact that his face twisted in pain and he caught at his left shoulder with his other hand.

I had no sense of direction. It was quite possible that I was traveling in a circle. Though it was growing dark, I could still see Enrique behind me. Then, over my right shoulder, I caught sight of B.J. fighting his way into the grove. He saw me, too, and with a yell he raised his hand. I saw the flash of his gun and heard the zing of the bullet as it grazed a tree trunk and ricocheted off into another. I felt as if someone had presented me with a gift, but B.J. cursed loudly and bitterly as he realized a bullet could never find a straight path to me. Resuming his blundering pursuit, he yelled, "For Christ's sake, Hank, get the lead out! If you let her get away," he gasped, "I'll get Immigration after you the minute I can get to a phone."

The threat sounded every bit as ominous to me as it must have to Enrique. I knew it would spur his determination to catch me. Raphaela had been awesomely frank about the lengths he was willing to go to in order to remain in the United States. But as I fought the trees, pulling myself around and between them, I compared our motivations. Formidable as his was, mine was stronger. Escape was a matter of life or death to me. Surely I had the edge.

One moment I was smothered by trees, the next I burst into open country with a star-studded sky overhead. Ahead of me, a quarter of a mile ahead, loomed a massive shadow I couldn't identify. Then the moon, which had been behind a wispy cloud, floated free and painted a round dome silver. It was Mission San Jose. And within its walls was Father Donahue, with a monastery filled with monks. The realization that help was so near propelled me forward like the thrust of a jet engine.

My pursuers broke into the open moments after I did, but I had used those moments well. By the time Enrique and B.J. burst out of the grove, I had covered half the distance to the mission.

It was only a short time before I realized that they were making the most of the open country, too. Even B.J. was moving with surprising speed. He would have to answer to Nell and Elliott Stansbury if I got away. He had deserted his post and left me alone while he went to dinner, reason enough for his desperate pursuit of me.

I was in the open now and plainly visible. If he wasn't shooting at me, it was because he didn't want the monks to hear. My lungs were burning, and the stitch in my side returned. I calculated the distance to the wall of the mission compound. The length of a football field maybe. I could do it. I could!

The yellow stone wall was gray in the moonlight. I hurled myself against it at a point where the black shape of a tree hovered above it on the other side. My bare feet sought and found footholds among the mortared stones, while my hands clutched and grabbed and pulled my weight upward. At the top I found myself on the roofs of the old Indian quarters. Crouching, I scurried along them to the tree and shinnied down it. Once on the ground, I headed toward the monastery, which was located at the rear of the compound. The brick path felt soft as a carpet compared to the rough ground I'd covered on my way.

Someone else was running across the roof. My

eyes frantically sought a hiding place. The doors of the Indian apartments were closed. I tried two. They were both locked. Now the footsteps were on the path. As I ran, I kept to the shadows cast by the living quarters. In front of me loomed the dark mound of an oven, with its darker mouth. I stopped and bent down. The opening was too small. I sprinted to the next one and, flat on my stomach, managed to wriggle through the low opening. The interior of the oven was pitch-black. It was so small that I barely managed to get into it. My knees were folded sharply against my chest; my back was pressed against the rock wall. The smell of soot was still incredibly strong after two hundred years, and my nose twitched like a rabbit's. I had to press a finger across my upper lip to stop a sneeze.

Footsteps padded by. I heard a shout. Enrique, who must have been standing next to the oven, gave an answering shout. I felt as well as heard B.J.'s thudding footsteps as he came running up, wheezing and coughing. "Where'd she go?" he gasped.

"I do not know, señor. I saw her running along here, and then she disappeared."

"Christ! You didn't let her get to the monastery, did you?"

"I don't think so, señor. If she had run in that direction, I'm sure I would have seen her."

"Then, where'd she go?"

"She must be hiding."

"You know this place?"

"Of course, señor. My wife and I attend mass here."

"Well, I was only in here once, and that was a long time ago. Where could she hide?"

"The old Indian quarters, the old mill, the church itself..."

As he ticked off the possible hiding places, I fought the convulsive shudders that shook my body and set my teeth to hammering. I was soaked with perspiration from running, and now the sharp night air and the cold rock that pressed against my back chilled me through and through. My teeth were chattering so loudly that I fancied the sound would roar up the small chimney and give me away. The sound of B.J.'s wheezes were coming to me as if through a megaphone. He must have been standing directly above the chimney.

"I don't know where any of those things are," he was saying. "I'll go to the gate that leads to the monastery and make sure she doesn't get to it. You look for her—and, Hank, you'd better find her."

The thud of his heavy steps receded, and for a long moment I heard nothing except my body twitching against the stone wall of the oven. Then I heard the whisper of Enrique's coveralls as he set about his search. There was the rasp of a door being pushed open. Fortunately I had not found that unlocked door, or I'd have hidden there only to be flushed out by a desperate man.

A few minutes later the door was pulled shut again and the next one tried. Among the possible hiding places, Enrique had not mentioned the ovens. Apparently he assumed that no one was small enough to crawl through these small openings. I hoped he wouldn't remember my size.

As the sounds he made in his search gradually

faded away, I began to consider my situation. I was horribly uncomfortable and shivering uncontrollably. And I couldn't count on remaining undiscovered. The stakes were too great for both Enrique and B.J. I *had* to be found. Sooner or later, when I failed to turn up in any of the more obvious hiding places, they would remember the ovens. In another thirty or forty minutes, my hiding place would become a trap. Now that I was cut off from the monastery, there was no sense waiting here. But where could I go? The police? The idea was laughable. After the farcical performance Friday night at Elliott Stansbury's house, I could imagine their reaction when I showed up in soot-stained pajamas. They would never believe my story. I could see them shaking their heads when I told them that I had escaped by hiding in one of the two-hundred-year-old ovens at the mission. After a bland and sympathetic denial by Elliott Stansbury, they would send me to the nearest psychiatric ward.

There was only one person in San Antonio I could call for help—Joe. Whatever connection his father had with Elliott Stansbury, Joe himself would be willing to help me. He had made that clear yesterday. Somehow I had to get out of the mission and to a phone. Beyond the opposite wall of the compound ran a main thoroughfare. Surely somewhere beside it I would find a phone booth. I'd have to beg a dime from a passerby.

I waited until I was fairly sure that Enrique was so far to the rear of the compound that he couldn't hear me; then I started to slither out of the oven. As soon as I got my head out, I looked around as best I could. Enrique was not in sight. Inching all the way out, I crouched behind the oven and peered about. Enrique was just disappearing around the corner of the church, perhaps on his way to the old mill. I stood up, my knees cracking after being held in one position so long, and half staggered, half ran back to the spot where I'd come over the wall.

After I climbed the tree, I crept over the narrow roof and dropped to the ground on the other side of the wall. Pain shot upward from my blistered feet. Gritting my teeth, I ran around the corner and headed for the highway. The traffic was heavy at this early evening hour, and the lights from the cars held me in an almost steady beam as I made my way along the edge of the road. In my soot-stained pajamas, I felt as conspicuous as if I'd been stark-naked. I prayed no police car would happen along. I jumped when a car behind me honked, but it sped by, and I blessed the driver for his indifference. At the moment the only person I trusted to help me was Joe. I didn't want to be picked up by some well-meaning person who might decide the kindest thing he could do was take me to the police.

I caught sight of a phone booth. It stood about a block ahead of me at the corner of a busy fast-food drive-in. As I limped toward it, a car pulled up beside me and someone asked, "Hey, can we give you a lift?"

The car was a beat-up red Mustang. The driver and his friend looked about sixteen or seventeen. They probably thought I was their age. "No, thanks," I told them. "I'm only going as far as that phone up there."

The boy in the passenger's seat looked down at

my feet and said, "You look like you could use a ride."

"I'm fine. Thanks anyway."

Their eyes lingered on me a moment longer, then the car shot forward and turned into the drive-in parking lot.

The closer I got to the phone booth, the more I limped. It was the letdown, I guess. The adrenaline wasn't pumping as fast as it had been when I was being pursued. I figured it would take Enrique and B.J. some time to conclude that I was no longer on the mission grounds.

When I reached the booth, I cast around for the right person to ask for a dime. I could see the red Mustang parked in one of the slots at the side of the building, but all I wanted was a dime—no help, no questions, no trouble with guys looking for a little fun. One of the carhops caught my attention: a dark-haired girl, tall, with broad shoulders and long legs. She moved easily and efficiently, and there was a cool, unflappable air about her. I limped a few yards toward a car where she was delivering a tray. "Would you give me a dime to make a phone call?"

She came toward me, taking in my bedraggled look unblinkingly. She fished a dime out of her pocket. "Here you go. Good luck."

"Thanks." Clutching the dime, I hurried to the phone booth and looked up Joe's number. After dialing, I scrunched down in the phone booth so I couldn't be seen from the outside. There were five rings before someone answered. It was Isabel.

"Is Joe there?" I asked.

"He's just leaving."

"Try to stop him, and hurry, please. Tell him it's Libby Kincaid."

The other end of the line fell silent, but I knew she was still there. "Please," I pleaded. "It's terribly important that I talk to him."

"One moment."

It was more than a moment. I waited an agonizingly long time, wondering if Isabel was making a real effort to intercept Joe and call him to the phone. Two faces appeared above me, grinning through the glass. My two friends from the red Mustang. I ignored them and fixed my eyes on the gum wrapper in the corner of the booth.

After a few moments one of them said, "Doesn't look like your party is going to answer."

"If you need a ride someplace," the other one offered, "we'll take you."

Concentrating on the phone, I prayed for Joe to answer.

"Libby?"

"Oh, Joe." At the sound of his voice, I almost lost control of my own.

"You can't be in New Orleans already. Where are you?"

"I'm here in San Antonio down the road from Mission San Jose. Two men dragged me out of my hotel room last night and took me to Elliott Stansbury's house. I've just now managed to escape. Can you come and get me?"

"I'll be right there. Tell me where you are."

I gave him the name of the drive-in and told him I'd be hiding in the phone booth.

"I'll be there in twenty minutes," he said and hung up.

I stood up, shaky with relief, and replaced the phone on its hook. Over at the corner of the parking lot a flash of orange caught my eye. It was Enrique. I ducked down, heart pounding. "Go away, please," I cried to my two young Samaritans.

"Hey, you talk funny! Where you from?"

"My father said he'd be here in five minutes. Now, will you leave me alone?"

"Your father, huh?" The driver pushed his glasses up on his nose and exchanged a glance with his friend. "And you call him Joe, right?"

"Sure. He never really wanted to be a father. He rejected the daddy bit from the start. Now, will you go away! You're attracting attention to me and"—I gestured toward my stained pajamas—"I'm not exactly at my best. Have a heart, fellas."

But they weren't giving up. They knew I was lying, and they were enjoying my predicament. One of them put his hand on the door as if to force it open. Suddenly, over his shoulder, the face of the carhop appeared. "Did you get your party?" she asked.

I nodded. "He'll be here to pick me up in twenty minutes. In the meantime I don't want to be seen, but these guys are complicating things."

"Bug off, fellas, and leave her alone," the girl said. Her tone was genial but authoritative.

"You just butt out, tall stuff. This is none of your business."

Her expression didn't change. She brushed back her long hair from her face and gazed toward the rear of the parking lot. "Look," she said to me, "my boyfriend is sitting over there in his car. He's alone. Why don't you wait in his car?"

I raised myself up just enough to look around. Enrique was nowhere to be seen. He'd either moved on down the street or returned to the mission. I stood up. "OK," I said and pulled the door open. Brushing past the two boys, who eyed us sullenly, we walked over to a yellow hardtop. The boys followed us until they got a good look at the fellow who was sitting behind the wheel. He must have weighed more than two hundred pounds and had a jaw as long as my forearm.

"Steve, can she wait in your car?" the girl asked. "Someone is picking her up in a few minutes, and she'd like to stay out of sight until then."

He got out and threw his seat forward. "Get in the back and lie down. If you tell me who to look for, I'll let you know when they drive up."

I turned to the girl before getting in. "Thanks." It was inadequate, but it was the best I could do.

She smiled. "Sure."

The two boys were walking slowly back toward the red Mustang. I climbed in the back seat and lay down. When Steve got back in, I said, "The man I'm waiting for is about twenty-eight or twenty-nine, black hair, lean, about five-nine or -ten. He'll go right to the phone booth, because I told him I'd be waiting there."

"OK."

"And if you see a Mexican in orange coveralls or a big, beefy man in brown pants and white short-sleeved shirt, let me know."

"Right. I don't see any of them right now." He didn't say another word until I asked his girlfriend's name a few minutes later. "Jan," he replied.

"She's a very special kind of girl," I observed.

"In every way," he said with quiet pride.

We lapsed into silence again. I lay there tensely, with butterflies in my stomach because I'd soon see Joe again. At the moment I couldn't think beyond that.

"There he is, the guy you've been waiting for," Steve said at last. "He's standing beside the phone booth looking around."

My heart gave a leap. "How about the other two men?"

Steve took a careful look around. "The coast is clear," he said as he helped me out of the car.

"Thanks, Steve, and thank Jan again for me, too."

He gave me a slow grin and nodded. I limped toward the phone booth. Joe saw me almost immediately and hurried forward. "My God, Libby! What have they done to you?" His voice choked.

My smile was shaky. "It's not as bad as it looks. Where's your car?"

He didn't answer; instead he picked me up and carried me to a car parked close to the booth. His arms felt hard and warm as they held me almost fiercely against his chest. It was all I could do to keep from breaking down as the fear drained out of me. He lifted me into the car and placed his jacket around my shoulders. As soon as he'd fitted his car into the traffic, he said, "Now tell me exactly what happened."

It was a relief to be able to pour out my story to him. He listened silently, his mouth grim. When I came to the part where I'd heard Nell and B.J. discussing my fate, he exclaimed, "Mexico! You're certain?"

"That's what they said. A man named Gomez

was to take care of me down there so that no trace of my body would ever be found."

A truck horn blasted behind us. Joe had swung out of his lane to pass the car ahead and hadn't seen the truck. He swerved back into his lane just as a semi came roaring up on his left. He let up on the accelerator, flexing one hand and then the other, as if forcing himself to relax. "Go on with your story." His voice was taut.

When I reached the part where I was slithering into the oven, Joe gave me an incredulous look. The ovens! But that's——" He broke off as his eyes swept over me. "Yes, I suppose you could have managed it." He shook his head and chuckled with genuine amusement. "No wonder they didn't find you."

"I was afraid they'd think of the ovens after they'd looked everywhere else. Sooner or later it would have occurred to them that I was small enough to crawl through one of the larger openings. That's why I got out of there and called you. I was afraid to call the police, afraid they wouldn't believe me. Let's face it, it's a fantastic story, and they've already heard me tell another."

Joe turned into the Contreras driveway and drew up before the front door. He helped me out of the car. As my mangled feet touched the asphalt, I moaned with pain. Again Joe swept me up in his arms and carried me into the house. Halfway through the living room we met Isabel, every gray hair in place, her gray uniform and white apron as fresh as if it were eight A.M. instead of eight P.M. I must have been quite a sight. The expression on Isabel's face was so funny I almost laughed.

"Where's my father?" Joe asked.

"He's in his office," she said slowly, still staring.

Joe pushed past her and carried me down a hallway past a dining room on one side, a library on the other, and opened the door beyond the library. I saw a large square room as featureless and austere as a monk's cell. The walls were painted pale green, and a worn gray carpet covered the floor. The room was furnished with a large metal desk, a couple of gray filing cabinets, a black plastic-covered couch and three straight chairs. Faustino Contreras sat behind the desk, facing the bare wall to his left. He didn't appear to be doing anything except staring at that blank wall. As we entered, he turned his head but, except for the flicker of his dark eyes, his melancholy expression did not change.

Joe laid me on the couch and spread an afghan over me. Then he went over to his father's desk. Until that moment neither man had said a word. Now Joe announced, "Here's your cargo. What the hell do you plan to do with her now?"

## CHAPTER NINE

My reflexes had slowed from those of a hunted animal to one who had reached the safety of her lair, and so I lay motionless for a moment while my mind tried to grasp this sudden shift in my situation. My sensual perceptions were unnaturally sharp. I was all too aware of the pain in my feet. I smelled the smoke and after-shave fragrance that lingered in Joe's jacket, which I still held around my shoulders. I saw the muscle in Joe's smooth cheek twitch as he stood tensely before his father. And I saw Faustino Contreras sitting there stolid and heavy as a pre-Columbian statue.

Then my reflexes snapped to life, and I was off the couch and sprinting past Joe toward the open door. He flung out a hand to catch me, but his fingers barely grazed my arm. I didn't feel the pain in my feet as I ran down the hall and into the living room. Behind me I heard Joe call my name. At the sound of his voice saying my name, the reality of his betrayal struck me like a blow, and I stumbled. I fell, still ten feet from the door. His hands closed over my arms. I fought wildly and had almost managed to tear loose when he pinned me to the floor, his body on top of mine.

"Libby, listen to me! It's all right. Calm down!"

"You're all in it together! I should have gone to the police!"

"I won't let anything happen to you. No one's going to kill you." His face was inches from my own. "I won't let anyone touch you!"

He meant it. I began to cry. Joe pushed my hair gently back from my face and brushed my cheeks with his lips as he murmured soothing words. At last, when I had quieted, he picked me up and carried me back into his father's office. Faustino Contreras hadn't moved. He still sat at his desk. Only his eyes seemed alive.

This time Joe, still holding me in his arms, stood in front of his father and told him, "You've got to go to the police."

Faustino Contreras regarded us for a long time without speaking. The only sign of any emotion was the deepening of the lines that ran from his nose to the corners of his mouth. It was as if an invisible sculptor were chiseling them ever deeper. Still without speaking, he left his chair and pulled out a drawer in one of the filing cabinets. He took out a bottle and a glass and poured himself a drink. His hand was shaking. He swallowed the drink quickly and set the glass on top of the cabinet, leaning against the cabinet as he did so, his head bent.

"You know I can't go to the police," he said at last.

"You've got to, Dad. This is murder."

Faustino Contreras whipped around and went back to his desk, declaring, "There won't be any murder. The girl is safe now."

"Yes, thank God, but you were ready to deliver Libby to the killer. Dad, not even Laura Lynn's happiness is worth that!"

"Not to you, maybe," Faustino Contreras snapped. "You're in love with this girl, it's obvious. Suddenly she means more to you than your sister. Well, she doesn't to me!" He strode back to the file cabinet and brought the bottle and glass back to his desk. "Put the girl down. If you're trying to arouse my pity, you're wasting your time."

Joe moved toward the desk until it was pressing his legs. "Look at her. Goddamn it, I said look at her! I don't give a damn for pity. All I want from you is a sign that there's still a small spark of humanity left inside you. Is guilt the only emotion you can feel anymore? Are you so corroded by it that you would help someone kill another human being?"

"Shut your mouth. You won't talk to me like that. Not ever again, do you hear?"

"I'll talk to you any way I please until something I say shocks you back into the real world. I know what these last four years have been for you. But if you think you can make everything up to Laura Lynn by agreeing to whatever Stansbury wants you to do—even murder—you're crazy. That's all Laura Lynn needs—a murderer for a father."

His last shaft hit the mark. Faustino sank, gray-faced into his chair.

But Joe didn't let up. "If you make this flight tonight, there's no guarantee that there won't be another and another after that. Stansbury said he'd turn the negatives over to you, but you've got no guarantee. You might prove too useful to him."

"You want to see your sister ruined?" Faustino Contreras asked hoarsely.

"Maybe it wouldn't have to be that way. Maybe the police could handle it so that no one would ever find out."

"And what if they couldn't?"

Joe's voice was as hoarse as his father's as he replied, "What's more important, Laura Lynn's reputation or another girl's life?"

Faustino Contreras looked at me for the first time. I have never seen so much pain in anyone's face. He lowered his head as a great tearing sob shook his powerful shoulders.

Swiftly Joe turned and carried me out into the hall, bellowing, "Isabel!"

She appeared almost at once from a room farther down the hallway.

Joe said to her, "Draw a hot bath for Libby and then find her some clothes." He paused. "And take good care of her, Isabel. She's in this with the rest of us now."

She must have wanted to ask a dozen questions, but all she said was, "Come along, Miss Libby. You're going to be a hard one to fit, but I'll find something for you."

Joe set me down gently. His face was pale, and I could imagine what that scene with his father had cost him emotionally. "I'll see you in a little while," he said.

I limped along beside Isabel to a turquoise and white bathroom that made me feel as if I were walking into a swimming pool. She had me sit down on a gold metal stool upholstered in turquoise velvet. "You rest there while I run your bath."

"A hot tub sounds good, but I think I'd better use the shower instead," I told her. "My hair needs shampooing. I can smell the dust and soot in it."

"All right. Let's see. This is Laura Lynn's shampoo," she said, taking a tube from the medicine chest. "And here's an extra comb. The towels are there on the rack. Can I get you anything else?"

I noticed for the first time that she seemed very nervous. I wondered how much she knew. Then I recalled Joe's words when he told her to take care of me. It seemed that the Contrerases had no secrets from Isabel.

"You wouldn't have a spare toothbrush, would you?" I asked. "My teeth feel as if they were covered with flannel."

She handed me a tube of toothpaste and a new toothbrush, explaining, "Laura Lynn's friends never bring toothbrushes when they spend the night. They can't be bothered with a little detail like that. So I keep extras on hand." She gave one last glance around and then left, saying, "I'll go find something for you to wear."

I smiled to myself. Despite her agitation, I had no doubt that the ever-efficient Isabel would find something suitable for me to wear.

At first the hot water pelting against my raw feet was almost more than I could bear; then it began to feel soothing. I luxuriated in the warmth and in the fragrant suds. I seemed to be scrubbing away the fear and evil that had clung to me for so many hours. I had just draped one towel around my middle, having wound another, like a turban, on my head, when Isabel knocked and called from outside the door.

"Come in."

She entered the steamy bathroom with the folds of a red and gold print draped over one arm. "It's my caftan. It will do for now. I'll hang it on this hook. And these knit slippers should fit. I've got the coffee on, and I'll make some sandwiches. Kitchen's through the dining room."

"That sounds heavenly," I said, although I hadn't realized until then that I was hungry. "I'll be right in."

When my hair was combed and I'd slipped into the caftan, I examined myself in the full-length mirror on the door. Isabel had worked a miracle. I lifted the hem of the caftan and discovered that she had taken it up four or five inches. She must have run it up on the sewing machine while I was showering.

Although the door to Faustino Contreras's office was closed, I could hear the murmur of voices as I passed by on my way to the kitchen. Isabel was waiting with the coffee and sandwiches on a tray. After a quick, critical glance, she nodded her approval. "That's better. Let's go into my sitting room. We'll be more comfortable there."

The sitting room, which adjoined the kitchen, was a homey, restful room. A chair and footstool stood close to a small TV set. Over in one corner was the sewing machine, still uncovered, with a spool of red thread on the spindle just as she'd left it. On a table beneath a window was a picture of the Contreras family, taken while Joe's mother was still alive. Through an open door I could see the adjoining bedroom.

"Take that chair." Isabel pointed to the chair with the stool. After I was seated, she pulled up the coffee table and then another chair and set the tray on the table between us. Her hands were trembling slightly as she poured us each a cup of coffee and offered me the plate of sandwiches. "There's ham and chicken. Eat all you want. I like to see people eat. Laura Lynn has this idea that she's too heavy, and she's always dieting. Eats nothing but a dab of this and a dab of that. I scold, but I don't get anywhere. Faustino is on her side. He bought the material for her dress for the debutante ball and a size-ten pattern. She's been size twelve for two years, and she looks fine to me. I'm making the dress, and if that pattern gains a bit in the cutting, neither of them is going to be the wiser."

"Have you been with the Contrerases a long time?" I asked.

"From the beginning. I worked for Melissa's family before she married Faustino." Her voice tightened a bit. "When she left, I left with her. I had loved her since she was ten years old. I helped raise Joe and Laura Lynn, and when Melissa died I went on taking care of them and of Faustino, too. They're the only family I've ever had."

"Joe told me about Melissa's father," I said. "And he told me about her death."

There was a pause. When Isabel spoke, it was

with difficulty. "Melissa was very warm, very loving. We all miss her very much."

She sat quietly for a moment, turning her cup on its saucer. When she spoke, her voice was tinged with sadness. "The children have adjusted much better than Faustino. Sometimes I think the only thing that keeps him going is Laura Lynn. He doesn't have to worry about Joe anymore. Joe can run the business as well as his father. But Faustino is obsessed with seeing that Laura Lynn moves in the same social circles her mother did and that she makes a good marriage. Without Melissa, it hasn't been easy. Some of the old friends fell away." The bitterness in her voice told me why—the running sore of prejudice, which nothing, it seemed, would ever heal. Upon Melissa's death, the doors that had once been open to Faustino Contreras were abruptly closed.

"After the accident," Isabel went on, "Laura Lynn grew quieter, more mature. I think she spends too much time alone, always reading. She's got several friends she seems to feel close to, but she's not a good mixer. And then there's her limp. She does most everything other girls her age do—plays tennis, dances. Actually, to see her on the dance floor, you wouldn't know one leg was shorter than the other. The same with swimming. But when she walks away from the pool or off the dance floor——" Isabel shook her head. "Although she's got some friends who are boys, she doesn't really have a boyfriend. Faustino frets about that, though he never says anything to her. He wants her to have a normal life—husband, children." Isabel sighed. "It's going to be harder for her than for other girls.

"That's why when this queer thing happened to her, Faustino was almost beside himself." Isabel's voice thickened, and she had to pause briefly before she could continue. "We didn't even know she had been kidnapped until that man Stansbury called and told Faustino to come and get her. You see, she sometimes goes to her friend Pat's house after school and stays for supper. She usually calls us, but sometimes she doesn't. She figures we'll know where she is."

Isabel passed the tray of sandwiches to me again, but I protested, "I've already eaten three."

"Three halves," she reminded me relentlessly. "That's only a sandwich and a half. Here, have another chicken. It's white meat and low on calories, if that's what you're afraid of. I've learned a lot about calories since Laura Lynn's been dieting."

Although I wasn't really hungry, I took another sandwich, hoping she would tell me more about Laura Lynn's kidnapping while I ate. She did. She talked about it as if she believed Joe had told me everything and there was no need to conceal her opinions. But, as it turned out, she didn't know the full story.

"When Faustino brought Laura Lynn home, she could hardly walk. He told me she'd been drugged. I wanted to call a doctor, but he said no. He said she would sleep it off and be all right in the morning. He made me promise not to say a word to anybody. If I did, he said, it would cause a scandal that would ruin Laura Lynn's life even though she had done nothing wrong. Her kidnapping must remain a secret among us three. Laura Lynn was never to know the truth. He would make up a story to tell her. He couldn't go to the police, he said, so he'd have to handle it himself. The look on his face when he said that sent shivers up my spine."

Isabel paused and poured herself another cup of coffee, as if to dispel that chilling memory. "He told Laura Lynn that her kidnapping was the result of a business argument between him and Stansbury and that she wasn't to tell anyone, or he'd be ruined. You never have to tell Laura Lynn anything twice. I know she hasn't even told Pat—that's probably the only secret those two haven't shared. She's at Pat's tonight. Faustino wanted her out of the house and asked her to spend the night there. I could see Laura Lynn suspected something, but she's not one to argue. Faustino isn't going to get into any trouble, is he?"

The question took me by surprise, and I stammered, "Why I—that is, I don't know."

"I shouldn't have asked. If he wanted me to know what he was doing, he'd have told me."

"Isabel, I'm not keeping anything from you," I assured her gently. "I honestly don't know. When Joe told you I was in it with the rest of you, he didn't mean that he had told me the whole story." Then I told her about my own kidnapping and how I'd managed to escape. "Whatever it was Faustino was planning, he changed his mind when he found out it involved a murder. I believe he's decided to go to the police."

Maybe she had heard the scene between Joe and his father, or maybe she hadn't. The office door had been open, and she very well could have. In any event, I saw no reason to mention how Faustino had at first refused to go to the police.

For a moment Isabel looked relieved; then she asked with some concern, "What will that mean to Laura Lynn—the scandal, I mean?"

"I don't know. Joe and his father appear ready to take the risk that the police can keep it from becoming known."

Isabel shook her head, and her face puckered in consternation. "I don't understand it. Laura Lynn's a good girl. She wouldn't do anything wrong."

"Isabel? Libby?"

Joe's voice brought Isabel instantly to her feet. She opened the door to her suite. "We're in here," she said.

The door opened into the hall. Joe entered and stopped just inside the room. His eyes sought mine with an eagerness that brought a flush to my cheeks. "You're looking better," he said, but his look said more. "I see Isabel is taking care of you. Food and Band-Aids are number one and two on her list of first-aid treatments."

"They've worked on you, haven't they?" she retorted. "You're tough as a Longhorn steer."

"Isabel is a wonder," I told him, still feeling the warmth in my cheeks. "She's made sure I have everything I need." I glanced at the tray of sandwiches. "And more."

Joe laughed, but there were lines of strain around his eyes. "I'm glad she's taking charge, because I've got to leave for a while. I'm driving Dad to the police. I have no idea when we'll be back."

"I'll be fine. Don't worry."

"I'll see you later, then," he said quietly. His look sent the kiss he couldn't give me while Isabel was there observing us.

* * *

Joe and his father were gone for two hours. Isabel turned on television, and we watched a suspense movie that was so lacking in real terror that I fell asleep.

I was awakened by a hand grasping my shoulder. For an instant I imagined I was bound and gagged in that dusty bedroom in Elliott Stansbury's house. But when I turned my head, I saw Joe gazing down at me.

"How do you feel?" he asked.

"Fine," I replied. I sat up quickly and looked around for Isabel. She was nowhere in sight, but I could hear her moving around in the kitchen.

Joe explained, "She's making a pot of coffee for us. Dad's waiting in his office. He wants to apologize to you and try to explain." He held out his hand to me. I stood up, and we walked down the hall to his father's office.

He was seated behind his desk, staring at the wall. But this time, when he turned toward us, his face was not the cold, stiff mask that he usually wore; it was a face that revealed how emotionally drained and tired he was. But strong. He was a man still very much in control of himself and the situation.

"I realize that no apology from me could ever make you forget I was willing to go along with a plan to kill you," he said after Joe and I were seated in two chairs drawn up in front of the desk. "For the last few days I've been out of my mind. If it hadn't been for Joe shocking me back to reality——" He broke off and looked down at a small manila envelope he was holding in his hands.

Beside me Joe made a fist with his right hand and

pounded his knee—once, twice, with such a strange slow motion that I glanced upward at his face. His cheek dimpled as he clenched his teeth. His eyes were fixed on the envelope in his father's hands.

"Joe has persuaded me to tell you the whole story. He tells me that your relationship with our family is going to be a permanent one and that it is essential that you understand why I was—why I could even contemplate becoming involved in a murder."

I was still two sentences behind him, absorbing what he'd said about my future relationship with his family. But the word *murder* dissipated that delicious haze.

"You know, of course, about Laura Lynn's kidnapping, and none of us can ever thank you enough for trying to help her. I do regret having made her lie to you, but it wasn't an ordinary kidnapping. Elliott Stansbury wasn't interested in ransom. He wanted a pilot who could fly to Mexico and pick up a shipment of drugs. Someone fumbled last time, and the pilot he's been using is now under police surveillance. It was Nell Fincher who came up with the idea of using me. She and B.J. had worked for me for a short time several years ago. When I caught B.J. taking kickbacks from the company that sold me cement for my wells, I fired them both. It seems they were waiting to get even with me."

A shadow passed over his face. "They knew about the plane crash, of course, and about my attempts to make sure that Laura Lynn would have the same opportunities that she would have if her mother were still alive. I'm sure it was Nell's idea. She dotes on cruelty. She picked Laura Lynn up outside her school on Friday afternoon, told her that Joe and I were at Elliott Stansbury's house, that we were there signing some contracts and that she, as an heir, had to come along and sign them, too. Laura Lynn remembered only that Nell had once worked for me; she had no reason to suspect that anything was wrong. And since she turned eighteen, I've been registering some wells in her name. It seemed to make sense. So she walked right into it."

He fell silent and stared once again at the envelope he held in his hands. The room was absolutely still, but I felt something that prickled the hair at the back of my neck. The silence was finally intolerable. At last Joe said quietly, "Show her, Dad."

Faustino Contreras's face had gone gray. He pulled several photographs from the envelope. After shuffling through them several times, he handed one across the desk to me. Although I was warned by his ashen face and his trembling hands, I was still unprepared. It was a snapshot in hideous living color. I sucked in my breath, blushing furiously, and I handed it back, not looking at either man.

Faustino said hoarsely, "That's the least of them. The others are worse. They drugged her into insensibility and then posed these pictures. I don't know the man and woman."

Still not looking at either of them, I said, "They are Stansbury's servants, Enrique and Raphaela."

"By God, I'll see that they pay for this, along with Stansbury and the Finchers," Faustino exclaimed vehemently.

"Enrique and Raphaela are in this country illegally," I explained. "Stansbury could expose them at any time. Enrique is willing to do anything to stay here, and he's warned Raphaela that she has to do the same, because if she gets sent back, she goes alone. She loves Enrique so much that . . ." My voice trailed off.

"They're here illegally?" Joe repeated slowly and turned to his father. "That might be just what the police need to get into the house."

Joe hadn't finished speaking before Faustino had the phone in his hand and was dialing. He asked for a Lieutenant Burch and told him about Enrique and Raphaela. The conversation made no sense to me, but Joe was listening intently. When Faustino hung up, he looked at Joe. "They won't have any trouble getting in now." He glanced at the manila envelope on his desk and tapped it with a thick brown forefinger. Resuming his explanation to me, he said, "Stansbury still has the rest of the roll of these snapshots, and he threatened to send the pictures to the president of the Brackenridge Club unless I flew to Mexico and picked up a shipment of drugs that was coming in from France. He knows I fly down to Mexico regularly and that no one would suspect I was making this flight for him." Faustino Contreras tossed the envelope into a drawer and locked it. "I agreed to do what he said. I suppose," he said slowly, "I'm no different from this Raphaela. I was willing to do anything for the person I loved— even help with a murder. When Stansbury called me today and said that he was holding you in his house and that I was to take you to Mexico, I knew what it meant. To make sure I kept my word, he said he was calling Gomez with orders not to turn over the drugs to me until you were delivered to him. If I returned here without the drugs, these pictures—or rather those he was keeping—would go out to George McCorkle in tomorrow morning's mail. Mac is president of the Brackenridge Club."

He passed his hand over his face. "I didn't let myself think about anything but Laura Lynn and what would happen if anyone saw the pictures. I was out of my mind."

No wonder. Even if the truth could somehow have been told, the humiliation for Laura Lynn would have been devastating. She'd never have been able to face her friends again.

"That's the story," he said wearily. "An apology would be so inadequate that I won't make one."

"I understand how you felt," I said looking at Joe. *What hostages we are to love,* I thought to myself.

Joe caught my hand tightly in his and smiled. Faustino Contreras started to say something, but at that moment Laura Lynn came in and said, "Daddy, I——" She broke off when she saw me.

Faustino Contreras was on his feet immediately. "Laura Lynn, what the devil are you doing here? You're supposed to be at Pat's."

"Well, I . . ." She tore her eyes away from me and shifted them to her father.

"You remember Libby Kincaid," he said. "I've told her everything," he explained. "Joe and she—well, she may be a member of the family soon."

If Laura Lynn was surprised, she didn't show it. She had grown used to shocks and surprises these last few years. She gave me a rather strained smile. But I realized the strain had nothing to do with me when she turned back to her father and said, "I couldn't sleep. I was worried."

"About what, honey?" her father asked easily.

"Whatever it is you're going to do tonight. Daddy, you're not—I mean, this thing you're doing isn't illegal or something, is it? You've kept it such a big secret that I can't help suspecting it's illegal or terribly dangerous."

Faustino and Joe exchanged a look, and then Faustino said quietly, "It's illegal, honey, but I've just come from the police. I've told them about it, and they're going to take care of it."

"Well, then, can't you tell me what it is? Please?" She looked agonized. Her eyes pleaded with her father. "This has something to do with why I was kidnapped, doesn't it?"

Faustino Contreras's eyes went to the locked desk drawer where he'd placed the pictures. It was tell her part or tell her all. "Laura Lynn" he said, "the Finchers know how much you mean to me. They engineered your kidnapping so that Stansbury could show me how easy it would be to hurt you. He needs a pilot to fly to Mexico tonight to pick up a drug shipment and bring it back to him. He said if I didn't do it, he'd—well, he'd hurt you again, and much worse. I've told the police what I'm going to do; they're going to be waiting at Stansbury's house when I deliver the stuff to him. They'll get him, and I'll be in the clear. And I won't have to worry about him or the Finchers hurting you anymore."

"But you could get hurt yourself, even killed."

"Not likely. Stansbury and the Finchers aren't expecting any trouble. The Mexican couple who work for Stansbury are in the United States illegally. The police can persuade them to let them hide in the house until I arrive later tonight with the drugs."

"But there might be some shooting."

"If there is, they won't be shooting at me. I'll get out of the line of fire, don't worry."

"Are you sure, Daddy?" she asked doubtfully.

He got up and went around his desk to her. She was as tall as he was. He kissed her forehead and said gravely, "I'm indestructible. Nothing happens to me, only to those close to me."

They clung together, and then Faustino said huskily, "Now, go on back to Pat's. It's getting late. You should be in bed, and I've got to leave in a little while."

As she turned to leave, she said to me, "I guess I'll be seeing more of you."

"Yes, I'm looking forward to that."

She smiled then, a lonely smile. She gave Joe a hug and went out, back to her friend Pat, back to innocence—providing everything went according to plan.

## CHAPTER TEN

"Dad's due in Zacapa at two A.M. for the pickup, so he'll be leaving in about an hour. A mechanic is getting the plane ready now. It takes a little less than two hours to fly there, depending on headwinds."

We were seated beside the indoor pool. Faustino sat at his desk and consumed cup after cup of heavily sugared black coffee, waiting for the moment when he would leave for the airport. But Joe's tension demanded physical release, so he had suggested a swim.

I declined. "Not even Isabel could come up with a suit that would fit me. Besides," I added, "I've had enough exercise for one day. I'll keep you company, though."

The indoor pool was at the rear of the house, a concrete block addition with a high ceiling and two walls of windows. The walls had been painted with epoxy and shone like turquoise tile. The pool itself was thirty or forty feet long and at least half as wide. The perfectly clear water was as blue as the walls. A small dressing area had been built at either end, and several plastic chairs and lounges were scattered around the sides.

"Dad built it after the plane crash. He thought swimming would be good for Laura Lynn's leg, and it was one sport where her lameness would be no handicap. It's been great for her—and for her friends. Weekends are usually just one long swimming party around here. Actually, we all enjoy it, even Dad. I'll be out in a minute," he said, heading for the dressing alcove at the far end.

I sat down on an orange lounge chair and lay back. I was in a curious emotional state, euphoric, because I was in love and knew I was loved in return and because I no longer felt the terror that I'd endured almost from the moment I arrived in San Antonio. But I felt apprehensive, too. Despite Faustino's attempts to minimize it to Laura Lynn, I knew he was in very great danger. When Elliott Stansbury and the Finchers realized they'd been tricked, they weren't likely to give themselves up to the police without a fight. I couldn't imagine their being unarmed, and someone's gun was sure to be turned vengefully toward Faustino, unless the police moved very swiftly.

And there were those pictures of Laura Lynn. God forbid that anything should alert Elliott Stansbury before the police moved in so that he would make those snapshots public.

Joe waved at me as he emerged from the dressing room and then dived into the pool and swam half a dozen lengths. "Ahh," he groaned in satisfaction as he stopped just beneath the place I was sitting, "that feels great. Sure you won't come in? We don't have any rule here against skinny-dipping."

"Another time, maybe," I said, stretching out contentedly.

He grinned and took off again, his brown arms flashing above the blue water, his legs thrusting him from one end of the pool to the other with remarkable speed and smoothness. When he'd had enough, he pulled himself up on the edge of the pool in front of my lounge and flopped down on the chair beside me.

I handed him a large striped towel from the small pile that lay on a nearby table. "Where'd you learn to swim like that?"

He shrugged as he rubbed the towel against his dark hair. "I've been swimming ever since I can remember. I won some medals in college."

"Where'd you go to college?"

"SMU. I didn't want to go. I figured I could run the business someday without wasting time at college. But Dad insisted. He wasn't able to go to college himself, and he was determined that I should go. So I went. And he was right, of course. It's getting more and more difficult to compete in any field without an education. Besides, I enjoyed it. You know, I almost got married to a girl I met there."

Although I felt a painful twist, I managed to keep my voice quite calm. "What happened?"

"As it turned out," he said, drying his chest and arms, "it wasn't marriage she wanted. She only wanted the ritual that led up to it: the lavaliering, the pinning, the engagement ring. I couldn't see her hang-ups until we'd set the wedding date. Then she began to get very nervous. She found an excuse to put it off. Finally she set another date and the rituals began again—invitations, buying the gown, choosing attendants, being showered. But at the last minute she couldn't go through with it." He tossed the towel aside. "A month before the wedding, she wound up on a psychiatrist's couch. The wedding was off; all the gifts had to be returned. Within a year she was married to someone else. It lasted six months." He shrugged. "I was well out of it, though it took me a while to realize it. By then it was getting late."

I looked at him. "What do you mean?"

He grinned. "I'd forgotten that you were too young to know."

He took my hand and rubbed my knuckles with his thumb. "It seems there's a proper season to be married, a period during a person's life when marriage is almost inevitable. You meet someone, fall in love and get married. It falls roughly in the early twenties. Once that time is over, it's harder to work things out. Anyway, my near miss has left me a bachelor long after most of my friends have been married."

"It appears I owe a great big thank-you to Miss What's-her-name."

"Me, too." He leaned over and kissed me.

A long time later I cleared my throat and asked, "Shouldn't we be getting back to your dad? It must be nearly time for him to leave."

Joe released me reluctantly and said, "I'll get dressed."

We found Faustino Contreras in the living room,

sitting in front of the TV set, which was spinning out a late movie. But he wasn't watching it. His eyes were fixed on the family portrait above the fireplace. He had lighted only one lamp, the one on the table beside his chair, and the portrait was shadowed but visible. Pain lay heavily on his mouth.

"Where's Isabel?" Joe asked as we entered.

Faustino gave one last look at the portrait and then shifted his eyes to us. "I ordered her to bed. She'd have stayed up all night if I hadn't, and she was exhausted. I told her it would be all over by six o'clock tomorrow morning, and there was no need to worry. She left a fresh pot of coffee in the kitchen."

"I'll get it," I said and left the two of them alone.

The light was on in the hallway, and I was guided through the shadowy dining room by a faint glow from the kitchen. Isabel had left the fluorescent light on the stove turned on. The percolator was still plugged in to keep the coffee hot. I found some mugs in one of the cabinets. While I was searching for a tray, I heard first Joe and then Faustino raise his voice. My heart sank. Although I wasn't able to make out what was being said, it was obvious that they were arguing. I found the tray Isabel had used for my sandwiches and carried the full mugs into the living room. Faustino was still in his chair, but Joe was standing in front of the fireplace. As I came into the room, he turned his head toward me and shouted, "Run, Libby! Get out of here!" Caught completely by surprise, I froze and stayed where I was, still clutching the tray. Then I heard another voice that sent the coffee tray crashing from my slack hands to the floor.

"Don't move, any of you!"

In the shadows beyond the glow of the single lamp, I saw a swift movement as B.J. pulled a gun from inside his jacket. The silence was broken by my small cry. My eyes flew to Joe in terror. He stood awkwardly, as if he had started toward me and then been frozen by B.J.'s warning.

"I tried to warn you," he groaned. "Couldn't you hear me?"

Through stiff lips I said, "I thought you and your father were arguing."

"Well, little Miss Small Town," B.J. sneered. "Fancy meeting you here. And all dressed up for a party, too. Sorry to spoil your fun." To Faustino he said ominously, "Elliott isn't going to like this at all."

"My bargain was to go down and pick up a package of drugs," Faustino said with surprising calmness. "It was Stansbury who threw in murder as an extra. When Libby turned up here, I saw no reason to notify Stansbury. I am still prepared to do exactly what I agreed to do originally, but I won't be a party to murder."

"You'll do anything the boss tells you to, buddy," B.J. said, his snarl more pronounced than usual, "unless you want those pretty pictures of your kid spread all over town."

"You filthy bastard," Joe said in a tight voice. His dark eyes flashed with fury.

B.J. turned the gun slowly until it pointed to the middle of Joe's chest. "You want to say that again?"

As Joe opened his mouth, I cried out for him to

keep quiet. Faustino's roar was even louder. "Joe! Save the name-calling until later!"

B.J. asked suspiciously, "What do you mean, later?"

"After I've got the drugs and delivered them to Stansbury, Joe can call you anything he likes. If your boss keeps his word, I'll have all the pictures by then."

"Yeah, Junior," B.J. agreed, "let's replay this name-calling bit then, OK?"

Through clenched teeth Joe said, "I can't wait."

They glared at each other silently for a moment before B.J. said, "Where's your phone?"

Joe didn't reply. Faustino gestured toward a green phone on a table in the corner. Motioning Joe to the chair beside his father, B.J. said, "Sit there. You, Miss Small Town, sit on the floor at his feet."

We did as we were ordered, and Joe laid his hand on my shoulder. It was blessedly comforting, although I knew he was equally helpless at the moment. With his gun pointed toward us, B.J. went to the phone and dialed.

"Elliott, this is B.J. Guess what I found at the Contreras house. . . . The Kincaid girl. . . . Hell, no, he wasn't going to say a thing. . . . Well, I was giving him your last-minute instructions, and in walks the girl. She's all cleaned up. Looks like she's been here quite a while. . . . Don't worry, I'll see that she gets aboard the plane. . . . What? Now, wait a minute, Elliott. You know I hate to fly. I . . ."

He listened for a while, and when he spoke again there was an edge of panic in his voice. "I can't do it, Elliott. Honest to God! *I can't fly!*"

He began sweating. A rivulet ran down past his

ear and hung beneath his jaw. "He won't try anything, Elliott," he insisted. "He knows what will happen if he doesn't do exactly what you say. . . . Jesus, Elliott. . . . Yeah, I hear you." His voice had thinned, and the habitual snarl was absent altogether. "OK." He hung up and glared at us. "It looks as if I'll be going to Mexico with you. You son of a bitch," he said fervently to Faustino, "Elliott doesn't trust you now. I've got to go along and see that there's no hitch." He looked around the room frantically. When he saw the bar, his relief was almost comical. "You," he said, gesturing with the gun at Joe, "get me a drink. Bourbon."

As Joe walked toward the bar, B.J. called, "Bring the bottle." He wiped his steaming face on his jacket sleeve and asked, "How long does it take to fly from here to Zacapa?"

"Two hours," Faustino replied, "give or take a little."

B.J. had moved closer to us, so that the light shone on his face. All the color had drained out of it, and he was breathing very fast. I recalled that on the night I had dinner at the Stansbury house, Nell had taunted B.J. about his fear of flying. Now it pleased me to know that B.J. was every bit as frightened as I was.

"Hurry up with the bourbon, damn it! Set it here on this table. Now, go back and sit down."

Joe took his time returning to the chair behind me. The expression on his face frightened me. I shook my head in warning, but he looked right through me and sat down with stubborn slowness. B.J. poured himself a big helping of whiskey and drank it down in two gulps. After that he stood glowering at us for a full five minutes. No one broke the silence. Faustino sat absolutely still, never taking his eyes off B.J. I had seen all of B.J. I cared to and looked instead at the silky fabric that covered my legs, tracing the intricate paisley design with a forefinger. Behind me, one of Joe's feet bobbed in agitation.

B.J.'s voice sounded very loud when he finally spoke. "You're going, too," he said to Joe. "You'll be my insurance that your old man won't pull any stunts with that plane. He'll fly it nice and level or I'll put a bullet in your kneecap. Before I run out of kneecaps and elbows and suchlike, we should be back here safe and sound." His eyes began to search the room again. When he found what he wanted, he said to Faustino, "Cut the cords off those drapes and tie these two up."

Faustino got up without a word and got the cord. For the second time in twenty-four hours, I was bound, but only at the wrists. And B.J. didn't inspect the job. He was too busy gulping down the whiskey, nerving himself for the flight that lay ahead.

"OK," he growled when Faustino had finished. He looked us over. Joe and I were standing side by side, our hands tied behind us; Faustino was a few feet away. "I'll say this once," B.J. said. "There won't be a second warning. If you," he said, addressing Faustino, "try any tricks at all with that plane, Junior here is going to get it. And if the girl isn't delivered to Gomez and the drugs brought back to Elliott exactly as agreed, those photos are going to be dropped in a mailbox. And as for you"—he gestured toward me—"I'd as soon deliver you dead as alive, so don't try to escape a second time."

There was hatred in his white face. "All right," he concluded, picking up the whiskey bottle, "let's go."

We drove to the airport in B.J.'s car. Faustino was at the wheel with Joe beside him. B.J. sat in the back, directly behind Joe, with me on his left. B.J. lowered his window and sat there sweating. I saw his fear in his trembling hands that moved continually, wiping his face, raising the brown cigarette to his mouth, and then the bottle. As we rode on in silence, I felt as if I'd spent half my life being driven through the dark hours of the night to my death. I stared at the back of Faustino's head, broad and almost square, ears lying close to his skull. Joe's head was smaller, narrower, heart-wrenchingly dear. Tears stung my eyes. There was so much life still to be lived!

I wasn't aware we were approaching the airport until I saw a plane rise from the darkness and take off over our car. Faustino drove directly to an area where dozens of small planes were lined up on a concrete apron. As we got out of the car, B.J. looked us over and told Faustino to put his jacket over my shoulders to hide the obvious fact that my hands were tied behind me. He put his own jacket around Joe. "OK, let's go."

Faustino led the way down a row of planes to a red and white one. B.J. brought up the rear, and when we reached it, his breath whistled through his teeth and he exclaimed in dismay, "Jesus, it looks like a toy."

It was indeed small, smaller than the crop-dusting plane a friend back home used to take me up in. A strong crosswind would give B.J. the ride of his life. Faustino kicked the chocks away from the wheels before unlocking the single door, which was located on the passenger side. "How do you want us to ride?" he asked, flipping a switch that filled the cabin with dim red light.

"Huh? Oh." B.J. licked his lips. "We'll ride like we did in the car."

"OK. Libby, you'll have to get in first."

That meant putting one foot on a small step built on the side of the plane and pulling myself up to the second step on the wing. I couldn't do it with my hands tied behind me. B.J. lifted me roughly, and Faustino, standing on the wing, steadied me and helped me into the cramped space of the cabin. There were four seats, two in front, two directly behind, and less elbowroom than I had in my small sports car. Once I was stowed, Faustino announced to B.J., "You're going to have to ride in the copilot's seat."

"The hell I will."

"Either that or you're going to have to untie Joe's hands so he can climb in himself. You won't be able to get in that rear seat if you put him in front."

"I'm not untying him, and I'm not leaving him out here alone while I climb in. He'll ride in the back."

There was a short silence during which Faustino stood waiting on the wing. I couldn't see Joe and B.J. from where I sat, but I heard B.J. muttering, "I'm going to make damn sure you don't work loose, Junior." When I heard Joe swear, I could almost feel the cords cutting as B.J. tightened them around Joe's wrists. There was a great deal of grunting as Joe was boosted up to the wing and steadied by his father. He crawled awkwardly into the seat beside me, and Faustino, working with difficulty in the crowded cabin, started to fasten Joe's seat belt.

"What the hell are you doing?" B.J. asked suspiciously, climbing up to the wing.

"Fastening their lap belts."

"Leave it. I'll do it. I want to make sure they stay put."

Faustino lifted one shoulder and slid into the pilot's seat without another word. B.J. bent almost double to get through the door and settled heavily into his seat. It took a lot of reaching and twisting, but he managed to fasten our lap belts so tight that, with our arms behind our backs, we were almost totally immobilized. Meantime, Faustino was going down his checklist. When B.J. was securely strapped in his seat, Faustino said, "Pull the door closed," and then reached over and locked it himself. "All set?" he asked, glancing back at us. Joe nodded his head. B.J. took a swig from his bottle and wiped his other hand across his brow. "How about you?" Faustino asked.

"Get going," B.J. replied hoarsely, "but remember, no stunts." He lifted his right hand so we could see the gun.

It was a macabre scene: the men's faces—and mine, I suppose—grotesque masks in the red glow of the instrument panel. Faustino turned the switch, and the tiny cabin exploded in sound. I could feel the rough throbbing through my seat. He brought the radio microphone to his mouth, but the engine was making so much noise I couldn't hear him or the replies from the control tower. We began taxiing out of the small parking area toward the runway. We passed an airliner being prepared for a flight at its loading gate, and B.J. stared at it, turning his head as we went by. We looked like a moth darting past an eagle. "God!" I saw B.J.'s lips form the word as he was reminded of how small our plane was.

I was no more eager to take off than B.J. was. Although it had been far from peaceful and only briefly pleasant, San Antonio seemed like paradise now. Hell lay in Mexico. In much too short a time we were positioned for takeoff. The seats were anchored to the cabin floor by a steel frame. As the plane picked up speed, I saw B.J. stash the whiskey bottle hastily in his lap and grab hold of the frame, his right hand clutching the bar between his legs, his left hand taking a grip between his seat and Faustino's. As the runway lights fell away below us, he closed his eyes. And when Faustino went into his turn, B.J. gave a queer strangled sound. "Take it easy, you son of a bitch!" His voice was a thin soprano.

"I've got to make my turn," Faustino replied, peering steadily through the windshield. "I've got——"

B.J. interrupted, still in that high voice, "I don't want a goddamn flying lesson! If you've got to turn, do it easy."

Faustino shrugged and said, "OK," and put the plane into a slower turn.

B.J. dropped his head and fixed his eyes on his lap to avoid being reminded by the lights below that he was in the air. We had flown in silence for fifteen or twenty minutes when he complained, without raising his head, "Christ, it's hot in here! Can't you give us more air." He loosened his hold one hand at a time and wiped his palms on his trousers.

Faustino had already opened the outside vents, and the night air made the cabin uncomfortably cool for me. Isabel's caftan was made of thin jersey, and the jacket that Faustino had thrown over my shoulders had slipped off and lay bunched between my back and the seat.

"I've got all the vents wide open," Faustino explained.

"Well, turn on the air conditioner."

"I don't have one."

B.J. raised his head a couple of inches to sneer, "I thought you were a rich man. Can't even afford a plane with air conditioning. You have to fly a goddamned toy."

Faustino turned his head and took a long look at B.J. huddled beside him with a grip on the seat frame that must have been bending the bars. "You ought to be glad it's so small. With a grip like that you just might manage to hold this one in the air."

B.J.'s reply was a string of obscenities that Faustino, busy flying again, didn't seem to hear. When B.J. finally ran down, he lapsed into silence, wiping his sweating palms now and then on his trousers. No one was inclined to break the silence.

The fear I'd known as a prisoner in Elliott Stansbury's house seemed in retrospect only a minor discomfort compared to what I was experiencing now. I was only two hours away from a fate that B.J. had sadistically hinted at. If Joe hadn't been there beside me, I'm not sure I could have retained a wisp of sanity. But his presence, helpless as he was, provided an icy determination on my part to live—no matter how impossible escape seemed at the moment.

"How much farther?" B.J. asked, breaking the long silence. His normally fleshy face had a pinched look.

"We're about halfway there," Faustino replied. He took a cigarette from his shirt pocket and said, "Hand me my lighter, will you? It's in the pocket of my jacket."

B.J. glanced at him, then back at me, and immediately dismissed the idea of giving up his grip on the seat. I wondered if Faustino had asked for the lighter simply to call attention to B.J.'s terror and humiliate him. B.J. apparently suspected the same thing, because he fumbled around for a book of matches from his own shirt pocket and tossed them into Faustino's lap. "Take these, you goddamned spic." He took a hasty pull from his bottle and grabbed hold of the seat again. The rush of air through the vents brought the stink of his sweat back to me. I hadn't seen his gun when he brought out the matches or when he took that drink. A man in his condition should be easy to overpower, if only Joe and I could get loose.

Beside me I could see Joe twisting his arms, trying to loosen his bonds and wincing from the pain. It was a futile struggle. When B.J. tied you up, you stayed tied. I tested my own bonds. They were tight. The thin drapery cords were tough and securely knotted. But I was hopeful: I'd managed to get loose once before. I began working my wrists, straining against the cords. The noise of the engine covered the sound of my uneven breathing, or so I thought.

"Hold it, Miss Small Town," B.J. shouted. I

froze and glanced up. He was peering at me through the narrow space between the two front seats. He had the gun pointed straight at my heart. "You're not getting loose this time," he declared. "It's only because I think Gomez will prolong the job a little longer than a bullet that I'm denying myself the pleasure of shooting you, but don't tempt me. If I catch you working those ropes again, I'm going to cheat Gomez out of his fun."

All my anxiety had been focused on what was going to happen to me when we landed in Mexico. Now I was reminded that death was much closer. It waited only a few feet away in that crowded airplane. I stopped trying to slip out of my bonds.

## CHAPTER ELEVEN

After B.J.'s threat, I lapsed into a stupor. Death seemed inevitable. There were one or two moments when I even welcomed it as a release from the fear that held me in its nauseating grip. I was only dimly conscious of Joe's renewed struggle against his bonds. He was wasting his time, I knew, and after a while he realized it, too. His head fell back against the seat in defeat, and he grew very still.

Beyond the window there was nothing but blackness. It was so thick and heavy we didn't seem to be moving at all. We were just hanging there, dangling from an invisible wire. I don't know how long I sat there paralyzed by despair, but all at once I felt a warm breath on my cheek, and Joe's lips moved against my ear. He was leaning across the few inches that separated us. "Cheer up," he said. "I've got a plan."

He spoke in a nearly normal tone, and my eyes flew to B.J. to see if he had heard. But the roar of the engine covered Joe's voice. His face had lost its frozen look; and his eyes were shining through the eerie light. My heart gave a small leap, and when Joe saw that he had brought me back to life, he leaned toward me again. "I'll never get my hands free, but maybe I don't have to. Can you see the gun?"

I shook my head. We could both see B.J.'s left hand clamped around the steel frame in the space between his seat and Faustino's. But not even from where I was sitting could I see his right hand.

Joe said, "He couldn't have it in his hand and still grip the seat like that. It's either in his lap or down on the floor next to his hand."

I nodded in agreement.

"If I threw myself against his seat and got him off balance, maybe Dad could grab the gun."

I turned and put my mouth to his ear. "You can't throw him off-balance," I said, "not while he's bracing his body that way."

"I know. I'll have to wait until he brings his right hand up to wipe it. Once Dad gets the gun, he can make B.J. do what we want. If he doesn't, we'll threaten to take him on a ride back to San Antonio that will drive him out of his skull."

"What will you make him do?"

"Untie us, for openers. As we land, Dad can get the plane into position to take off quickly and leave the engine running. While I hold the gun at his back, B.J. will get the drugs aboard, and before Gomez realizes what's happening, we'll take off with you still safe and sound in your seat."

It sounded much too chancy and dangerous. "What if Gomez has a gun and starts shooting?"

"I think we can count on that. We'll just have to trust to luck. The minute Dad starts taxiing for the takeoff, I want you to lean forward to make as small a target as possible." He paused; then his lips moved again. "It's dangerous as hell, but it's our only chance to get you and the drugs back to San Antonio."

And once back there I'd be safe, because the police would take care of Elliott Stansbury and remove that threat forever.

"Any comment?" Joe asked and leaned away from me.

"I love you," I said, forming the words silently with my lips.

He grinned and then placed his mouth against my ear once more. "OK. I'll make my move the next time B.J. raises his right hand."

We waited. Faustino flew the plane in remote silence. His withdrawal was so complete that I felt he wasn't even there, that he had strapped his body into the pilot's seat and then gone off somewhere to let the plane fly itself. B.J. was silent, too, wrapped in his own excruciating terror, but his presence was a noxious and evil thing.

The minutes crawled by. I hadn't noticed when B.J. last dried his sweating palms, but surely it was time he did so again. I was staring fixedly at his back, when Faustino surprised me by turning to say something to Joe. Until that moment, he had not once looked back at us. His head gave a queer jerk, and then I saw his eyes start from their sockets. His mouth went slack, and before our horrified eyes he collapsed. His body fell forward against the control wheel. Abruptly, the plane nosed down, and B.J. screamed. Joe was on his feet in an instant, squeezing his body between the front seats and shouting for B.J. to cut him loose. B.J. either didn't hear or couldn't move. He sat there making sharp, strangled cries, his hands frozen to his seat. I stood up and leaned over Faustino's seat. I wanted to pull his body away from the control wheel, but with my hands tied behind my back, I was helpless. Again Joe shouted to B.J., "Cut me loose, you fool, or we'll crash!"

Slowly and with movements as uncoordinated as an infant's, B.J. took a knife from his pocket and sawed at the cords around Joe's wrists. The instant Joe's hands were free, he hauled his father's body away from the instrument panel. He held on to his father with one hand, while he pulled back the control wheel with the other. "Cut Libby loose," he ordered. "I need her help with Dad."

This time B.J. obeyed without delay. As soon as I was free, I pulled the weight of Faustino's body away from Joe and propped his body against the window. His head rolled back and forth. In the dim red light his face appeared lifeless. Pressing my hand against his chest, I felt a heartbeat and the rise and fall of his chest. "He's alive," I shouted to Joe.

"Thank God!" To B.J. he said, "Get in the back. Move! I've got to fly this plane."

Still making strange, barking cries, B.J. wormed into the seat Joe had vacated. He sat there gripping its metal brace, a strand of spittle dangling from his mouth. Joe eased himself into the copilot's seat. I felt the plane begin to climb. Faustino said something in Spanish. Joe answered him in Spanish, his tone gentle, soothing. Faustino did not seem to hear him; he went right on muttering.

"He thinks my mother is here," Joe said. His voice sounded flat.

"Jesus," B.J. sobbed. "What a time to die!"

"Shut up, Fincher. Sit down, Libby. I'm turning around. I've got to get Dad back to San Antonio to a hospital."

B.J.'s head came up. "The hell you do!" His words were strong, but his voice was weak. "You take this thing on into Zacapa or I'll shoot——"

Joe broke in. "You'll shoot nobody. I've got your gun." He held it up above his head for B.J. to see. "You forgot to take it with you when you changed seats."

B.J. licked his lips and said nothing for a moment. When he did speak, it was with something like his old snarl. "Listen, Junior, have you forgotten about your sister? You better get those drugs and take them back to Elliott, or she might as well be dead. We're almost there; it's not going to make that much difference. Your old man could just as well die if you turned around now. You want your sister to lose her father *and* get a name as a sex pervert?"

Joe flew in thoughtful silence for what must have been five minutes. Faustino continued to mutter. Now and then I could make out the name "Melissa."

"I'll make a bargain with you," Joe said finally. "I'll land at Zacapa, but you'll tell Gomez the situation has changed and you're not handing over the girl. Get him to give you the drugs, and we'll take off immediately."

"He won't let you get away with that," B.J. said scornfully.

"What'll he do, shoot me? Who would fly the drugs back to Stansbury? What's more important, killing Libby or getting the drugs over the border?"

B.J. had to think that over. Joe gave him all the time he needed. It couldn't have been an easy choice for B.J. Nell couldn't abide sloppy jobs. B.J. was no doubt quailing at the thought of returning with me and facing her contempt. Elliott Stansbury wouldn't be very happy about my return, either. Still, the original purpose of this whole filthy plan had been to get the drugs across the Mexican border and into his hands. They were probably worth millions of dollars.

"OK," B.J. said at last, "you've got a deal. But if you think Elliott is through with this kid, you're crazy."

Joe ignored the threat and issued one of his own. "When I land, I'll taxi into a takeoff position and leave the engine running. If you try any tricks, I'll take this thing right up again and give you a ride that will leave you in worse shape than Dad. Got that?"

B.J. licked his lips again. "Yeah."

"OK. Now, how do I find Zacapa?"

"How the hell should I know? The two times I've come here, it was by car. Doesn't your old man have some maps?"

"He didn't bring any. He told me he knew how to find it. Can't you give me something that will help me identify it?"

"It's just a town, for Christ's sake, full of spics

and flies and dogs. It looks like every other Mexican town I ever saw."

"Well, think, man! We should be almost there. Is there a river nearby, or a mountain?"

"Yes, mountains!" B.J.'s voice cracked in his relief. "It's in a kind of bowl with mountains all around. How you going to keep from running into them?"

"There'll be lights on top of them as a warning to aircraft. I'll go up to thirty-five hundred feet. I should see the lights somewhere ahead of us."

Faustino was droning on. Joe answered him gently in Spanish, and Faustino grew quiet. I felt the plane begin to climb, and I peered out the window. I saw nothing but blackness. Below us were those miles of Mexican desert where Gomez was to bury my body. I shivered and thrust my arms into Faustino's jacket, pulling it closely around me.

"Melissa, *querida.*" The tenderness in Faustino's voice brought hot tears to my eyes. What was it that had felled him—a stroke, a heart attack? Joe must be nearly out of his mind with worry. If there were a doctor in Zacapa, perhaps we could—but of course we couldn't, not without giving away the smuggling operation that was now so nearly completed.

"There they are." Joe's voice broke into my thoughts. "The warning lights. I'm beginning to see the lights of Zacapa, too. Now, where are we supposed to meet Gomez?"

"At his place. He's got his own landing strip. He lives a few miles west of Zacapa. That's all I can tell you."

I could see two red lights now. That was all. Then

Joe turned the plane a bit, and I could see a cluster of white lights ahead, like beads in a bowl, with the dark mountains enclosing them on all sides.

"That must be Gomez's landing strip. There. See?"

B.J. looked out the window and then dropped his head quickly. "If it's west of town, that's it. How many more minutes before we land?"

"We should be down in a few more minutes. I'm going to circle first and make sure I've got the right strip. Are there any other landing strips?"

"Christ, I don't know!"

"Well, I only see one at the moment. I'll circle and see if I can spot any more. We don't want to get the wrong one."

"Watch those goddamned mountains. I'd feel a helluva lot safer if your old man was flying this goddamned toy."

Joe's only reply was, "I'll set you down as soft as meringue, but don't forget, I've got the gun now. If you try to double-cross me, I can shoot a kneecap as well as you can."

"Just set this thing down, Junior, and I'll get the drugs aboard for you."

"OK, we're going down."

B.J. gritted his teeth as Joe put the nose of the plane down. The lights of Zacapa came up swiftly. It was a sharp dive—sharper than necessary probably—but maybe Joe wanted to hurry before B.J. could change his mind. Or maybe he felt B.J. deserved a little something extra.

I could see the runway now. It was no more than a tiny path lit by two parallel lines of light. My heart was beating rapidly. I didn't trust B.J., and I didn't know what we'd find on the ground. Gomez was a killer. Would he be alone?

The runway was just ahead of us now. The plane shuddered, and the engine noise roughened. B.J. yelled, "What's wrong?"

"Nothing's wrong. I let down the flaps to slow the plane so we can land."

I didn't realize we had touched down until Joe braked the plane and it began to bump along the unpaved landing strip. I could see the headlights of a car following us just beyond the line of lights on our left.

"There's Gomez," B.J. said. He had released his grip on the seat. Now that he was back on solid ground, his confidence had returned. You could see it in the way he sat, in the way he held his head, in the brutal set of his face.

"Now, remember," Joe warned, "Libby stays right where she is, and I'm taking off in ten minutes. So you better have the drugs aboard by then."

"Shut up, Junior. I know what I've got to do. Just stop this damned thing and let me get on with it."

Joe taxied to the end of the runway and turned the plane so that it would be ready for immediate takeoff; then he brought it to a stop without cutting the engine. We waited as the car pulled up on the other side of the lights. Two men got out and walked over to the plane. They were both Mexicans, short, square. Both had paunches. They wore dark suits and ties. Tweedledum and Tweedledee. When they reached the plane, Joe turned and pointed the gun at B.J.'s kneecaps between the seats. "You ready?" he asked.

"I'm ready, you bastard."

Joe unlocked the door and swung it out.

"Gomez?" B.J. called.

"Yeah." The man peered in. "Is that you, B.J.?"

"Yeah. Elliott sent me along to make sure everything went OK. Where's the stuff?"

Instead of replying, Gomez pointed to Faustino and asked, "Who's that guy?"

"That's Contreras. He had a heart attack or something a little while ago. Thank God I brought Junior along. He can fly, too."

"Is that the girl?" Gomez asked.

My heart skipped a beat. What would B.J. say?

"Yeah, that's her. Give me the stuff."

Gomez turned toward Tweedledee and snapped an order in Spanish. When Gomez again filled the doorway, I could see an attaché case in his left hand.

"Take it, Junior, and hand it back to me," B.J. ordered. As Joe reached for the case, B.J. threw himself against the back of Joe's seat and shouted to Gomez, "Put a gun on him, Gomez, but for God's sake don't kill him!"

At that moment, incredibly, Faustino moved. So did the plane. Gomez yelled as he lost his balance and disappeared. Joe thrust B.J. away from him and pulled the door shut. The plane picked up speed. B.J. lunged for Joe again. There were shots from outside, and B.J. fell back into his seat. At that moment the plane wobbled and dipped sickeningly. It was obvious we were in the air.

B.J. squealed and grabbed hold of his seat. "You bastards!" he whined. "You tricked me!"

They certainly had, and they had fooled me, too, so skillfully that I still couldn't fully realize that Faustino was not only alive but the picture of strength and alertness. As he made the turn that would take us—all of us—back to San Antonio, I leaned forward and said with undisguised amazement, "Faustino, you're all right!"

"Of course! I'm fine! Faking that attack was the only way I could think of to keep B.J. from getting you off the plane. I hoped we could get the drugs aboard first and then take off before they knew what was happening."

I understood then some of the things that had happened. "While you seemed to be mumbling incoherently, you were actually explaining all this to Joe. And probably telling him how to find Zacapa, too."

Joe spoke up. "And assuring me he was OK. You can guess what a relief that was."

"Sons of bitches!" B.J. said bitterly.

I glanced at him for the first time since we had taken off and saw that he was hanging on to his seat with only one hand. His other hand lay in his lap, and I could see a dark stain on his shirt at the shoulder. "B.J.'s been shot," I exclaimed.

Joe started to lean back and take a look at the wound, but B.J. snarled, "Keep your hands off me!"

"Better let me examine that wound. It looks as if it's bleeding badly."

"It won't kill me. I'll still be alive enough to tell Elliott how you guys kept me from handing over the girl. He's going to be furious when he finds out she's back in San Antonio, and alive."

"The drugs!" I cried, remembering. "You didn't get them."

"Oh, yes, we did," Joe said and held the briefcase up for me to see. "I had it in my hands when B.J.

made his move, and I tossed it under Dad's feet."
He turned to B.J. and said, "You can forget about
Libby talking. We're going to be married. She'll
never breathe a word of any of this."

B.J. snorted. "If you think Elliott's going to buy
that story, you're just plain stupid, Junior."

If the police plan worked, I reminded myself
quickly, it wouldn't matter whether Elliott Stansbury
bought the story or not. *If* it worked. Neither Joe
nor Faustino said anything, but I was certain they
were thinking the same thing.

## CHAPTER TWELVE

The flight to Zacapa, filled with terror and struggle and horror, had seemed to take an age. On the return flight, time resumed its normal pace. Of course I was happy to be alive, but I wondered what the price of my happiness would be. Ahead of me Faustino carried the briefcase full of drugs, which represented only half the job he had been told to do. Beside him walked B.J., his gait unsteady after finishing a whole bottle of whiskey, his "nerve medicine." He held his right arm stiffly across his stomach. The wound must have hurt hellishly, and I could imagine the savagery of his thoughts. Nothing Elliott Stansbury could possibly do against the Contreras family would satisfy B.J.'s desire for revenge. Nothing would ever compensate him for Nell's scorn when she learned of his failure.

The patches of darkness on the concourse between the glaring lights confused my perception. I stumbled, and Joe threw an arm around my shoulders to steady me. "Are you all right?" he asked.

"I'm fine. But I'm so tired—I can't remember when I had a full night's sleep."

"It will all be over within a couple hours, and then we can all get some rest."

I felt his tenseness as he held me close to him. I knew he was obviously thinking of those two hours and all the things that could go wrong. I knew Faustino must be worried, too, not for his personal safety, but for Laura Lynn because of the photographs that were still in Elliott Stansbury's possession. I recalled with emotion her unexpected return that evening, how she explained that she'd been too worried about her father to sleep. I'd been so deeply touched by her fresh and lovely innocence when she left after being reassured that her father would take care of everything.

After more than four hours in that tiny cabin, B.J.'s sedan seemed as big as a yacht. I slid into the back seat with Joe beside me. Faustino got into the driver's seat, and when he switched on the lights, the glow that lit our faces was healthy and normal. I peered at Joe beside me, delighting in the brown planes of his face no longer stained that grotesque red. At first Faustino put the briefcase on the seat between himself and B.J., but before driving off he had second thoughts. Handing it to Joe, he said, "Maybe you'd better put this someplace back there."

This seemed to please B.J. "You don't trust me, huh?" He preened himself at this evidence that he was still considered a threat. No one had considered it necessary to hold him at gunpoint when we left the plane and walked to the car.

"You're drunk, and you're stupid, and those drugs are the only thing I've got to trade for those photos of Laura Lynn. I'm not taking any chances on losing them."

As Joe placed the briefcase on the seat between us, B.J. called Faustino a filthy name and said hoarsely, "If you think those drugs are going to get you those pictures, you're the one who's stupid. You messed up that deal when you brought the girl back from Mexico. You don't know Elliott." He chuckled. It was an ugly sound.

Faustino backed the car out of the parking slot without giving any indication that he had heard B.J.'s threat. Joe reached for my hand and held it firmly. But his hand felt cold.

The streets, even at four-thirty in the morning, showed some life. Although the houses were dark, I could see them, and the streetlights flicked by with hypnotic regularity. This was not the black, empty world of the air.

It was no longer necessary to shout in order to make ourselves heard, and when Faustino spoke to Joe over his shoulder, he spoke in a normal voice. "I'll drop you and Libby off at the house and then take B.J. and the drugs to Stansbury."

"You can drop Libby off," Joe declared, "but I'm going with you."

"No, you're not," Faustino told him flatly.

B.J. spoke up. "You aren't dropping that girl off anywhere. You're taking her to Elliott." I thought I heard a note of desperation in his voice.

"I'm delivering the drugs," Faustino said, "that's all."

"Look, unless you deliver the girl along with the drugs, you have less chance than a snowball in hell of getting those pictures." Yes, it had been desperation I heard in his voice. It was strong now, and I thought I understood. He had botched the job Elliott Stansbury had sent him to do. Nell would never let him live that down. But if he could hand me over to Elliott, even though I was still alive, he could garner at least a soupçon of approval.

"We'll see about that," Faustino replied.

"I'm going with you, Dad," Joe said again. It was easy to read his thoughts. He was thinking about the moment when the agents would spring into the room intent on taking Elliott Stansbury. He wanted to be there to protect his father if he could.

Faustino read his thoughts, too, and when he spoke, his voice was softer. "The best thing you can do is wait at home. If anything happens to me, Laura Lynn is going to need you. She mustn't lose both of us."

Joe didn't reply. His fingers wound in and out of mine as he weighed his choices. I stared out the window, hoping desperately he would do as his father wanted. I told myself I wasn't being entirely selfish. Faustino's argument had been painfully sound. If anything happened to Faustino and if those photos should be mailed, who but Joe could stand between Laura Lynn and the salacious whispers that would destroy her?

I don't know what Joe's decision would have been, because suddenly Faustino exclaimed, "What the hell is that car doing?" He was peering into the rearview mirror. Joe and I turned to look. "It met us just now and is turning around," Faustino said, watching it.

I saw the lights of a car swaying as it made a fast U-turn, and as it sped up beside us, I saw two people in the front seat.

"That's Elliott's car!" B.J. exclaimed.

"What the hell is he doing here?" After a quick glance at the other car, Faustino was concentrating on not colliding with it as it remained beside us.

"Pull over. Can't you see him motioning?" B.J. snarled.

Instead of pulling over, Faustino gave his car more gas. The other car dropped far enough behind to bring the front windows opposite mine. I had time to see that Nell was driving and that Elliott was in the passenger's seat before the car shot ahead of us. It whipped in front of us, stopping with a screech of tires. Faustino slammed on his brakes, throwing us forward in our seats. Before we'd recovered our balance, Nell was beside our car pointing a gun against the rolled-up window at Faustino's head.

B.J. fumbled his way out of the car. "What's up?"

"Where's the stuff?" Nell demanded. Elliott Stansbury was approaching us with brisk strides. He, too, had a gun.

"The stuff is in the back seat," B.J. replied. "But what are you doing here?"

It was Elliott Stansbury who replied. "Gomez called and told me what happened. I sent Nell out to mail the photos. When she came back, she called Enrique to put the car away. One look at his face told me that something was wrong. I got it out of him. There were four narcotics agents hidden in the house. Enrique told us where. After Nell and I took care of them, we took off. One of Nell's skydiving pilots is flying us to Mexico. Gomez can get us to South America from there."

"One of those pilots?" B.J. asked in dismay. "Jesus, we'll leave a trail as wide as the Milky Way. What's to keep him from talking when this hits the papers?" Nell looked at him as if he possessed subhuman intelligence, and he said quickly, "Oh, hell! "I guess I lost more blood than I thought."

Until then neither Nell nor Elliott Stansbury had noticed he was wounded, but it wasn't his wife who asked, "What happened?" It was Elliott Stansbury.

B.J. explained and twisted his arm in front of the headlights to examine it. "One of Gomez's bullets got me. It's sore as hell, but it's stopped bleeding now."

"Where's the stuff?"

"Junior's got it."

"What's he doing here?" Elliott Stansbury asked, peering into the back seat.

B.J.'s tone was defensive. "I took him along for insurance. I didn't want Contreras doing stunts with the plane."

"Fool!" Nell spat at him. "No wonder you had trouble."

"Be glad I did!" B.J. snapped back. "Otherwise Gomez wouldn't have tipped you, and you'd never have known you were being set up."

B.J. didn't often have moments like this when he was right and Nell was wrong. Elliott Stansbury backed him up. He's right, it was a stroke of luck."

B.J.'s chest puffed up visibly. He even seemed to grow taller. Nell said acidly, "Well, are we just going to stand here talking all night? I thought we had things to do."

"And so we have, my dear," Elliott Stansbury said calmly. "Get out of the car, all of you."

As we obeyed, B.J. said, "Give me the briefcase, Junior, and my gun."

Joe handed over the gun and the drugs, and we stood there with our backs against the car. I was in the middle, with Faustino on my right, Joe on my left. There was a gun pointing at each of us. The carefully detailed plan the police had laid out to capture Elliott Stansbury was shattered. Somewhere in that hooded, evil house, four narcotics agents lay dead, and I had no illusions about what lay in store for Joe and his father and me.

To Faustino, Elliott Stansbury said, "You should never have brought the police into this."

"I couldn't be a party to murder."

For the first time since I'd met the man, Elliott Stansbury's voice held a note of anger. "So much for paternal love."

A strangled sound came from Faustino's throat, and he started for Elliott Stansbury but stopped in midstride as all three guns swung to him. In a choked voice he asked, "What would you know about paternal love or any other human emotion?"

In the glow from the headlights of both cars, I saw Elliott Stansbury smile thinly. "What's so virtuous about feeling emotion? Life is much more comfortable if one lives by reason. I chose not to wallow in the messy emotional life most of you lead."

"And where has your nice tidy, sterile life gotten you?" Faustino asked, his voice husky. "Police on your tail, fleeing the country, hiding for the rest of your life."

"You make it sound so unpleasant, so difficult, so painful, but you're wrong. I've enough money deposited in banks around the world to allow me to live exactly as I please. I don't anticipate any problems. The problems will all be back here when the right people see those pictures of Laura Lynn."

I felt sick, as if the blood had all drained to my feet, but Faustino said evenly, "I don't think that's going to be a problem. By the time this story hits the papers, the police will have explained to George McCorkle and the debutante committee, and the pictures will be destroyed."

"But I also mailed some to Laura Lynn."

Faustino's body sagged and shrank as the full import of Elliott Stansbury's words soaked in. "You bastard!" There was a sob in Faustino's voice. "I'll see to it they're burned the moment they're delivered."

"You won't be around to protect your daughter, Contreras, and you know it. As for the police taking care of Laura Lynn—do you really think they can protect her from the scandal those photos are going to create? Even if it's explained how and why the pictures were taken, no one who sees them is going to forget what they saw, least of all your daughter."

I thought Faustino was going to collapse. So did Joe, I guess. He made a move toward his father but was waved back by B.J.'s gun. Faustino put one hand on the front fender to steady himself and said heavily, "Kill me if you feel you have to, but leave Joe——"

I didn't hear the rest, because my ears were suddenly filled with the sound of a siren. It was very near but still out of sight around the corner of the block where we stood. Almost at once I heard the car itself, the roar of its motor building as if the driver had suddenly stepped down on the gas. Our heads snapped toward the sound, and then Nell, moving with incredible speed, headed for Elliott Stansbury's car. Just as she reached for the door handle, a police car swung around the corner, capturing the entire tableau in the beam of its headlights. The driver seemed not to have known we were there. For a split second the cruiser continued toward us; then a foot jammed the brake, and the car skidded wildly to a stop. Blinded by the headlamps and the flashing red light, I couldn't see the policemen, but I heard them shout, "Police! Drop your guns! All of you!"

Nell ignored the warning and leaped into Elliott's car. Two shots rang out, and the horn began blaring. The rest of us had frozen when the lights caught us, but at the sounds of the shots, Elliott Stansbury came to life. I was nearest him, and he grabbed me, yanking me in front of him as a shield, and began backing toward B.J.'s car. B.J. stood there blinking, his whiskey-soaked brain unable to grasp this abrupt turn of events. He obeyed the order, dropping both gun and briefcase in slow bewilderment, and stood with his hands behind his head.

Elliott Stansbury's gun was pressed to my head; his left arm was across my chest. "I'm getting in this car and driving away from here," he shouted, "and I'm taking the girl with me. If you shoot, I'll kill her."

Faustino was still standing in front of the car door,

and Elliott Stansbury yelled at him to open the door and then get out of the way. I was off-balance, struggling to get my feet moving in rhythm with Elliott Stansbury's, but he half lifted me as he dragged me backward. I felt the gun at my temple, smelled the freshly laundered shirt cuff that was only inches from my nose. My right arm was free, and I flung it up instinctively in an attempt to right my balance. As I did so, it struck something hard in the pocket of Faustino's jacket, which I was still wearing. The lighter. I stopped trying to regain my balance, and as Elliott Stansbury hesitated at the open door of the car, I leaned against him, putting my hand into the pocket. I flipped open the lighter top. It had to work on the first try; I wouldn't get a second chance. I put my hand up near Elliott's left wrist and spun the wheel with my thumb. The wick caught, and Elliott Stansbury shrieked, flinging his arm straight out. I ducked and dived for safety toward Joe and Faustino. The three of us fled around the rear bumper as shots were fired.

I heard the sound of running feet but could see nothing. Joe had shoved me behind him, and the three of us crouched at the rear of the car. Then over Joe's shoulder I saw a policeman spin B.J. around and handcuff his hands behind his back. Joe helped me to my feet as Faustino stood up. I could see it all now. Elliott Stansbury was clutching his burned left wrist, when the second policeman ran up and handcuffed him. His face, spotlighted by the cruiser's headlamps, had lost its baby-pink hue and its serene expression.

Joe had pulled me into his arms. "Are you OK?" His voice was shaking.

"Yes."

"How about you, Dad?"

Faustino was leaning against the rear fender. He still looked ghastly, but his voice was strong as he said, "Laura Lynn will never see those pictures."

"Not now she won't, Dad."

"And I'll see McCorkle first thing this morning and explain. I pray to God I can get to him before the mail arrives."

One of the policemen was herding B.J. and Elliott Stansbury across the street to the cruiser. The other stopped at Stansbury's car and pulled Nell away from the horn. In the sudden quiet, I heard the sound of another siren in the distance. Porch lights were turned on up and down the street, and when people realized the shooting was over, they gathered on their front steps and lawns. We watched the police tuck B.J. and Elliott Stansbury into the back seat of the cruiser. By then the approaching siren was so loud we didn't try to talk. When the car pulled up behind the cruiser, two plainclothesmen got out and spoke to the uniformed officers. One of the new arrivals, a tall, thin man wearing a stetson, broke away and came over to us. "Are you folks all right?"

"Yes." Faustino introduced me. "This is Lieutenant Burch. He's the one Joe and I talked to earlier at police headquarters."

The lieutenant acknowledged the introduction with grave courtesy and turned back to Faustino. "When our agents didn't make their hourly report from the Stansbury house, we knew something was wrong. We drove out there and found them." His voice was hard with anger. "I figured Stansbury would try to get out of the country as quick as he could. We sent the message out on the radio and ordered the nearest car to the airport. I guess Sergeant Lowell was just a block away from here when he received the call. I headed straight for the airport when we left the Stansbury house."

"Stansbury mailed the photos," Faustino said, staring at the patrol car that held Elliott Stansbury and B.J. "He even mailed some to my daughter."

"Don't worry. We'll find them if we have to open every drop box in town."

This reassurance acted like a stimulant on Faustino. He pushed himself away from the car fender, and his square body drew together and hardened. "Is the woman dead?" he asked, nodding toward Stansbury's car.

"No, sir. Sergeant Lowell has called for an ambulance."

"What about Enrique and Raphaela?" I asked.

Lieutenant Burch turned his long, thin face toward me. "They're dead, miss. We found their bodies in the yard. They must have tried to run away after they betrayed our agents."

I stared at him with mute horror. Poor Raphaela. I must have made some sound, because Joe's arm tightened around me.

"We'll take you folks home," Lieutenant Burch said.

He and Faustino crossed the street to his cruiser. Joe and I followed. I could see the heavy, round head of B.J. through the rear window of the patrol car. Beside it was the sleek, silver head of Elliott Stansbury. As I started to get into Lieutenant Burch's car, I noticed a jasmine bush growing along the curb, softly illuminated by a porch light. It was green and full, its drooping branches thick with blossoms. I went over and buried my face in it.

"What are you doing?" Joe asked. "Those things don't have any smell."

"I know. Aren't they marvelous?"

When I straightened up, I found him regarding me with a queer look on his face. I gave him a reassuring, if unsteady, grin and cast one final look toward the patrol car ahead of us. Then I kissed Joe's cheek and slid into the back seat. I'd have a whole lifetime to explain.

# OTHER SELECTIONS FROM PLAYBOY PRESS

### BUT DON'T GO ALONE $1.50
KATHERINE COURT
Lindsay had come to Katmandu for adventure. After a series of terrifying "accidents," she is convinced she is a target for murder. Alone in a strange land, she could trust only one man—or could she?

### EVIL SIDE OF EDEN $1.50
SARA NORTH
After being tried for and acquitted of the murder of her husband and her daughter, Laura begins a new life in Hawaii, only to find that she can't escape the horrors of the past.

### AN IRISH AFFAIR $1.50
ANDREA HARRIS
In Dublin to interview the leader of the Irish Republican Army, reporter Alix Nilsson overhears a plot to kill a number of top-level government officials. But before she can report it to the police, she is abducted by a group of desperate men.

### A MATTER OF REVENGE $1.50
CHRISTY DEMAINE
When professional photographer Andrea Wayne meets Paul Hunter, she has no idea he is a hired assassin. As their love grows, Andrea finds herself drawn into a complex maze of international intrigue—and she is marked for murder.

## A MESSAGE FROM JULIE $1.50
SARA NORTH

Karen's young sister, Julie, is missing in New Orleans. When Karen sets out to search the French Quarter for her, she is unaware that she is being watched and followed and that others—with more sinister motives—are also looking for Julie.

## THE TOUCH OF EVIL $1.50
LYDIA COLBY

Annette marries the governor of California, whose wealthy stepfather wants to see him elected president of the U.S. But Walter is tragically shot down, and Annette's worst fears are realized when she faces her husband's ghost.

## WAIT UNTIL MIDNIGHT $1.50
VIRGINIA PITTINGER

Melissa Mavros leaves America to seek her family roots in Greece, where her romantic dreams are shattered when she becomes the pawn in a dangerous game of political intrigue.

## WHITE MIDNIGHT $1.50
CILLAY RISKU

Maija returns to Finland and to her grandfather, who is convinced someone is trying to kill him. She becomes a victim of sinister events, as well, and Midsummer's Eve, an ancient festival celebration, becomes a night of horror.

ORDER DIRECTLY FROM:

PLAYBOY PRESS
P.O. Box 3585
Chicago, Illinois 60654

| NO. OF COPIES | | TITLE | PRICE |
|---|---|---|---|
| \_\_\_\_ | C16436 | But Don't Go Alone | $1.50 |
| \_\_\_\_ | C16451 | Evil Side of Eden | 1.50 |
| \_\_\_\_ | C16492 | An Irish Affair | 1.50 |
| \_\_\_\_ | C16402 | A Matter of Revenge | 1.50 |
| \_\_\_\_ | C16429 | A Message from Julie | 1.50 |
| \_\_\_\_ | C16415 | The Touch of Evil | 1.50 |
| \_\_\_\_ | C16484 | Wait Until Midnight | 1.50 |
| \_\_\_\_ | C16400 | White Midnight | 1.50 |

*Please enclose 50¢ for postage and handling if one book is ordered, 75¢ if two to five are ordered. If six or more are ordered, postage is free. No cash, CODs or stamps. Send check or money order, or charge your Playboy Club Credit Key #_____.*

TOTAL AMOUNT ENCLOSED: $_____

Name _____

Address _____

City _____ State _____ Zip _____